The Quiet Discretion Mysteries

Books 1-3

Dead Quiet in Briar Hollow

Quiet Profits in Briar Hollow

DIGITAL

Bloodline Blush in Briar Hollow

CSD Digital Enterprises, LLC

Petra Shaw

A Note to the Reader

A Note to the Reader

Welcome to Briar Hollow.

This is a cozy mystery series set in a small town where secrets tend to linger—and sometimes, objects remember what people try to forget.

Each book in this series features:

• A complete mystery solved by the end of the story

• A quiet paranormal element rooted in intuition and emotional echoes

• A curious amateur sleuth, a watchful talking cat, and a town that prefers its truths kept tidy

• No graphic violence, no explicit content, and no gore

While there is an ongoing thread connecting the series, every book stands on its own and can be enjoyed independently.

If you enjoy mysteries that unfold quietly, reward attention, and leave room for reflection after the final page, you're in the right place.

Series
Introduction

The Quiet Discretion Mysteries take place in small towns where people mean well—and where that often matters more than anyone wants to admit.

These are not stories about chasing danger or forcing answers. They are about what happens when silence starts being treated as agreement, and restraint becomes a tool instead of a choice.

Clara Whitlock runs a small antique shop. She listens more than she speaks. She notices what others overlook—not because it's hidden, but because no one has asked the right question yet.

Each mystery in this series stands on its own. Together, they follow a larger pattern: how authority forms quietly, how harm is disguised as care, and what it costs to refuse escalation when escalation would be easier.

If you're looking for loud twists or fast judgments, these stories may feel different.

If you're interested in quiet tension, moral pressure, and the consequences of choosing restraint, you're in the right place.

This series is best read in order, but each mystery can be enjoyed on its own.

Box Set Table of Contents

Bloodline Hush in Briar Hollow

Dead Quiet in Briar Hollow

The Quiet Discretion Mysteries - Book One

Petra Shaw

CSD Digital Enterprises, LLC

Chapter One

Dead Quiet in Briar Hollow

Clara Whitlock opened *Second Chances Antiques* the way she did everything in Briar Hollow—quietly, carefully, and as if the town might be listening.

The old bell above the door chimed once, soft and polite, when she unlocked it. Dust motes drifted in the angled morning light like lazy snow. The shop smelled faintly of cedar, lemon oil, and time—time trapped in drawers and cabinet corners, time that clung to fabric and wood the way perfume clung to a scarf.

Clara liked that smell. It meant objects had stories.

She just didn't like how often those stories tried to crawl under her skin.

"You're early," said a voice behind her, bored and velvet-smooth.

Clara didn't jump anymore. She set her purse on the counter, flipped the *Closed* sign to *Open*, and glanced toward the old armchair by the front window.

Nimbus sprawled in it like he paid rent.

He was a black cat with yellow eyes so sharp they looked carved. His fur was sleek and tidy, his tail wrapped around his paws with the smug elegance of a creature who'd never once had to work for a meal.

He also talked.

Not to anyone else, thank goodness.

Clara hung her coat on the hook and lowered her voice on instinct. "I'm always early."

"You're always anxious," Nimbus corrected. "There's a difference."

"Don't psychoanalyze me before breakfast."

Nimbus's ears twitched. "You don't eat breakfast."

"Don't start."

He blinked slowly, which in cat was either affection or contempt. With Nimbus, it was usually both.

Clara moved behind the counter and ran her fingers over the glass display case. Rings. Cameos. A handful of old watches that no longer told time but still demanded attention. Antique stores were full of broken things, and customers came in hoping a little beauty could distract them from their own fractures.

Clara understood that better than most.

She opened the register, checked the change, then scanned her appointment notebook. Tuesdays were appraisal days. The kind of day where locals brought in attic clutter and called it "family treasures" with a straight face.

The kind of day where Clara's gift—if you could call it that—made itself everyone's problem.

It wasn't a psychic thing, not exactly. She didn't see the future. She didn't talk to dead people. She didn't swirl herbs in a bowl and chant. She did not, under any circumstances, do anything that would get her labeled as "one of those Whitlock women" the way the older ladies at church liked to whisper.

She just... felt things.

Not emotions in the air, not vibes, not whatever people on the internet called it. Objects held on to moments the way cloth held on to smoke. And sometimes, if she touched them wrong, those moments bled into her.

A ring could hum with devotion. A child's toy could prickle with grief. A kitchen chair could press her ribs with an anger so old it felt like a bruise.

Most days she managed it. Gloves. Breathing. A light touch. Quick appraisals. Short contact. Let the story stay in the object. Let it be somebody else's burden.

Nimbus watched her like a judge waiting for a defendant to slip.

Clara pretended she couldn't feel his gaze.

The bell chimed again at nine fifteen, and in walked Vesta Rowe, wearing her favorite purple cardigan and the tight expression of a woman who'd practiced holding her life together for so long she didn't know how to stop.

Vesta had lived in Briar Hollow since before Clara was born. She organized the volunteer bake sales. She had opinions about potholes. She had a son Clara went to school with, a husband who'd died young, and a way of looking at people like she could see their weak seams.

In her arms, she carried a small wooden box.

Clara's mouth went a little dry.

Nimbus didn't move, but his tail flicked once. Like a warning.

"Clara," Vesta said, as if they hadn't spoken just two days ago. "You opened on time, at least."

"Good morning to you too," Clara replied, forcing a smile. "What have you got there?"

Vesta placed the box on the counter with care, as if it were something fragile or it might bite. "Family piece."

Clara didn't reach for it. Not yet. "All right. Want to tell me about it first?"

Vesta's fingers hovered over the lid, then pulled back. "It belonged to my father. Then my brother. Then—" Her mouth tightened. "Now it belongs to nobody."

Clara's stomach sank. "Is this about Travis?"

Vesta's eyes sharpened. "You heard."

"It's a small town," Clara said softly.

"That's the problem." Vesta's voice was controlled, but not calm. "Everybody's got a story about why my brother isn't answering his phone. Everybody's got a theory. Everybody's got something to say about the Rowes."

Clara kept her hands on the counter. "I'm sorry."

Vesta exhaled through her nose. "Don't be sorry. Be useful." She slid the box closer. "He left this with me last week and told me to bring it here. Said you'd know what it was worth."

"I can appraise it," Clara said carefully. "But if he's missing—"

"He's not missing." Vesta said it too fast. Too hard. "He's... Travis."

Clara bit down on the reply that wanted to come out: *That's not an explanation.*

Instead she said, "Okay. Let's take a look."

Nimbus rose from the chair, stretched, and hopped onto the counter with the casual entitlement of a creature who believed surfaces existed for his convenience.

Vesta's gaze snapped to him. "That cat again."

"He lives here," Clara said. "In spirit."

Nimbus yawned, showing a pink tongue and sharp teeth. "I prefer to think of it as reigning."

"Mm-hm." Vesta's eyes narrowed. "Still talking?"

Clara's spine went cold.

Nimbus froze mid-tail-flick.

Clara forced a laugh that sounded like it belonged to a different person. "Not in any way that would matter."

Vesta stared at Nimbus a moment longer, then looked back at Clara. "Fine. Appraise the thing."

Clara didn't like how that moment had felt—like a trapdoor creaking, like the town noticing her in a way it usually didn't.

She reached for the box.

The moment her fingertips touched the wood, a thin thread of sensation slid up her arm.

Not bad. Not sharp. Just... old. Varnish. Dryness. A hint of tobacco and oil and a man's hands.

She exhaled slowly. "Okay."

She lifted the lid.

Inside was a pocket watch nestled in velvet that used to be red and had faded into the sad color of dried roses.

The watch itself was silver, heavy, well-made. Its face was covered, the casing etched with a delicate pattern that looked like wheat stalks and tiny flowers.

Clara's pulse thumped once, louder than it should have.

Nimbus's ears flattened.

"Don't," Nimbus murmured under his breath. "Don't do it bare-handed."

Clara's skin prickled.

She didn't have gloves on. She should have reached for them. That was the rule. Always the rule.

But Vesta was watching, and Clara didn't want to look strange. Didn't want to look like she was *afraid* of a simple object.

She told herself it was just a watch.

She lifted it.

The world snapped sideways.

A burst of emotion hit her like a hand around her throat—panic, raw and breathless, the kind that made lungs forget how to work. The pressure of darkness. The scrape of something tight and unyielding. A frantic thought, not words exactly but the shape of terror:

No no no—

Her knees wobbled. Her fingers spasmed. The watch clanged against the counter.

Clara sucked in air that felt too thin.

Vesta jerked back. "Clara?"

Nimbus's paw shot out and covered the watch like he could smother the feeling. His eyes were wide now, pupils blown.

Clara's heart hammered against her ribs so hard it hurt.

She blinked, hard, trying to force the shop back into focus. The light. The dust. The gentle hum of the old ceiling fan. Her counter. Vesta's startled face. Nimbus's paw planted firmly on the silver casing.

The panic wasn't gone.

It lingered like a smell in the back of her nose.

Clara swallowed. "Sorry."

Vesta's mouth tightened. "You just dropped it."

"I—yeah. Slipped."

"Are you all right?" Vesta asked, but her tone was suspicious now. Like Clara had failed some test.

Clara forced her hands flat on the counter so Vesta wouldn't see the tremor. "I'm fine."

Nimbus leaned in toward her, his voice low enough only she could hear. "That's not an heirloom."

Clara's throat closed again. "It's a watch," she whispered.

Nimbus's tail lashed once. "It's a warning."

Vesta's eyebrows pinched. "What?"

"Nothing." Clara pasted on another smile, one that made her cheeks ache. "Just... talking to myself."

Vesta looked unconvinced but let it go. "So? Worth anything?"

Clara stared at the watch like it might bite her.

There were rules about this. *Echoes* could come from anything: love, grief, anger. But panic that sharp, that choking, that immediate—

It wasn't nostalgia.
It was a moment preserved in metal, *like a fly trapped in amber.*

Clara steadied her breathing. She reached behind the counter, deliberately, for a pair of thin cotton gloves. Pulled them on one finger at a time.

Nimbus didn't move his paw until she nodded at him.

With the gloves on, Clara picked the watch up again.

The emotion was muted—still there, but buffered. Like listening through a wall.

She flipped it over. Ran her gloved thumb along the hinge. Examined the etching. Quality work. Possibly nineteenth century. Could be valuable to the right buyer.

But that wasn't what made her stomach twist.

"What did Travis say when he gave it to you?" Clara asked, keeping her voice casual.

Vesta's shoulders rose. Fell. "He said... 'If anything happens, take this to Whitlock.'"

Clara's breath caught. "He called me Whitlock?"

Vesta's eyes hardened. "He called you *Clara*, but he meant Whitlock. You know what people call you behind your back."

Clara did. She didn't need it repeated.

"And then?" Clara asked softly.

Vesta looked away, toward the window. "Then he said he was going to settle something. That he was tired of being treated like he didn't exist."

Clara's skin crawled beneath her gloves.

"Settle what?" she asked.

Vesta's mouth compressed. "I don't know. Travis doesn't tell me things. Travis decides and then expects everyone to deal with it."

Nimbus's eyes narrowed. "Travis Rowe is a walking bad decision."

Clara shot Nimbus a look. *Please do not.*

Nimbus licked his paw, utterly unbothered.

Clara cleared her throat. "How long has he been... not answering?"

Vesta's jaw tightened. "Since yesterday afternoon."

"And you're not worried."

"I didn't say that." Vesta's voice sharpened. "I said he's Travis. He's probably off with some woman or sleeping in his truck because he's mad at the world. He'll show up when he's hungry."

Clara's mind flashed to that burst of panic again. Darkness. Tightness. The scrape of something unyielding.

No no no—

Her stomach rolled.

She lowered the watch back into its velvet nest. Closed the lid carefully.

"I can appraise it," Clara said, and hated how thin her voice sounded. "But I'm going to need a day or two to research comparable pieces."

Vesta's gaze narrowed. "It's a watch, Clara. How hard can it be?"

Clara smiled again, small and polite. "Hard enough that I'd rather do it right."

Vesta huffed. "Fine." She reached into her purse and pulled out a folded slip of paper. "Here's my number. If Travis calls me, I'm going to scream at him. If you find out my father's watch is worth a fortune, I'm going to scream at him too."

Clara accepted the paper. Her gloved fingers crinkled it slightly.

Vesta picked up her purse and hesitated. "You're... you're not going to do anything stupid, are you?"

Clara's eyebrows rose. "Like what?"

Vesta's lips pressed thin. "Like go running around with your... feelings. Getting the whole town stirred up."

Clara held her gaze. "No."

Vesta looked like she didn't believe her, then turned and left.

The bell chimed behind her.

For a moment the shop was silent except for the faint hum of the fan.

Nimbus hopped down from the counter and prowled to the box. He sniffed it, then recoiled like it smelled wrong.

Clara pulled off her gloves with careful fingers. Her hands were still shaking.

"Nimbus," she whispered.

He didn't look up. "No."

"I didn't ask yet."

"You're going to," Nimbus said. "And my answer is no."

Clara stared at the box. The pocket watch sat inside, innocent as a sleeping insect.

"I felt him," she said quietly.

Nimbus's ears angled back. "You felt fear."

"I felt... trapped."

Nimbus finally looked at her, eyes like coins in the dim light. "Clara. People don't get trapped in pocket watches."

"I know." She swallowed hard. "So why does it feel like that?"

Nimbus hopped back onto the counter and sat, tail curled neatly around his paws. His voice dropped lower, the humor gone.

"Because something happened when he was holding it."

Clara's throat went tight again. "Travis is missing."

Nimbus's whiskers twitched. "Or he's about to be."

Clara's gaze snapped to him.

Nimbus held her stare without blinking.

Then he flicked his tail toward the closed box like a judge passing sentence.

"Put it somewhere you can't ignore," he said. "Because you're already involved."

Clara's hands moved on their own. She lifted the box and carried it to the locked cabinet under the counter—the one where she kept the valuables and the things she didn't trust.

She slid the box inside. Turned the key. Heard the soft click.

It didn't make her feel safer.

Not even a little.

Outside, Briar Hollow went on being Briar Hollow. Cars rolled past. A dog barked. The sky stayed bright and ordinary.

Inside, Clara stood with the key in her hand and the taste of panic still ghosting the back of her throat.

She could pretend it was nothing.

She could tell herself Travis Rowe was just being Travis Rowe.

She could do what everyone in town did when something felt wrong—look the other way until it became somebody else's tragedy.

Clara stared at the cabinet.

Nimbus watched her.

And somewhere deep in her chest, her own fear answered the watch's echo with a quiet, terrible certainty.

This wasn't over.
It was barely beginning.

Chapter Two

The Quarry Doesn't Keep Secrets

B riar Hollow didn't wake up so much as it *agreed* to be conscious.

The town made its decisions slowly—who to trust, what to talk about, which tragedies to absorb and which to pretend didn't exist. By eight a.m., most mornings, it had already settled into its familiar rhythm: trucks rumbling down Maple Street, a few early walkers circling the square, the bakery venting sugar into the cold air like a bribe.

This morning, the rhythm was off.

Clara Whitlock knew it before her phone rang.

Nimbus was still perched on the back of her kitchen chair, grooming with excessive precision, when the first call came through. Clara stared at the screen until it stopped ringing, as if the name could change if she refused to look long enough.

Vesta Rowe.

Nimbus didn't glance up. "If you ignore it, it doesn't count."

Clara exhaled and pressed accept. "Vesta?"

Vesta didn't bother with hello. "He's dead."

The words landed like a dropped plate—sharp, unmistakable, and impossible to gather back up.

Clara's hand tightened around the phone. "What?"

Vesta's voice sounded scraped raw, like she'd already said the sentence too many times. "Travis. They found him."

Clara's stomach turned cold. She slid into the chair as if her legs had forgotten how to hold her. "Found him where?"

"The quarry." Vesta's breath hitched on the word, then steadied into anger. "They say he fell. Like he just—like he just *tripped* and fell down there. Like my brother's an idiot."

Clara glanced at Nimbus. His ears were angled forward now, alert in a way that had nothing to do with curiosity.

Clara swallowed. "Who found him?"

"Earl from the sanitation crew. He was down there checking the old access road because kids keep sneaking in." Vesta's voice went brittle. "Sheriff Halden's already there. They won't let me go near him."

Clara's throat tightened. "Vesta, I'm so sorry."

"Don't," Vesta snapped. "Don't you dare give me that soft voice. I don't want your sympathy. I want somebody to tell me what happened."

Clara's gaze flicked toward the counter where she kept her keys. Toward the locked cabinet in the shop where the watch waited like a heartbeat.

Clara forced herself to keep her voice steady. "What are they saying?"

Vesta gave a humorless laugh. "What do you think? 'Tragic accident.' 'Careless.' 'He shouldn't have been down there.' Like it's the
quarry's fault."

Clara closed her eyes.

The echo from the watch rose up in her memory—panic, darkness,
pressure. Not a misstep. Not a slip. Something else.

"Clara?" Vesta said, sharper. "You're still there."

"I'm here." Clara took a breath. "Are you at home?"

"No. I'm at my sister-in-law's. People are... already." Vesta's voice
turned poisonous. "Already bringing casseroles. Already whispering."

Clara almost smiled at the bleak accuracy. Small towns didn't know
what to do with grief except feed it.

"I have to go down to the station," Vesta continued. "They want
statements. They want me to identify his jacket, his boots, like that's
going to make him more real."

Clara's fingers curled around the phone. "Do you have someone
with you?"

"Yes." A pause. "And no."

Clara understood. You could be surrounded and still be alone.

Vesta's voice dipped. "You... you didn't touch it again, did you? The
watch."

Clara's pulse stuttered. "Why?"

"Because Travis said something when he gave it to me." Vesta's voice
went quieter, and for the first time sounded scared instead of angry.
"He said... 'If I don't come back, Whitlock will know what to do.'"

Clara's mouth went dry. "He said that?"

"Yes." Vesta swallowed audibly. "So tell me. Do you know what to
do?"

Clara stared at the wall across from her where a patch of sunlight
warmed the paint like nothing had happened.

"I don't know," she said honestly.

Vesta's breath shook. "Then figure it out."

The line went dead.

Clara lowered the phone to the table and sat very still.

Nimbus hopped down from the chair and padded over, soundless as shadow. He jumped onto the table and sat close enough that his shoulder brushed her forearm. It was almost comforting, if you ignored that his comfort came with teeth.

"So," Nimbus said, calm. "Now we're in it."

Clara's voice came out thin. "We're not in anything."

Nimbus stared at her as if she'd said the dumbest thing he'd ever heard. "A man is dead, the watch screamed in your hand, and you're pretending this is a normal Tuesday."

Clara's throat tightened. "They said he fell."

Nimbus blinked once. "People say a lot of things because it's easier than admitting they missed something."

Clara pushed back from the table and stood. The chair legs scraped the floor, loud in the quiet kitchen. "I'm going to the shop."

Nimbus's tail flicked. "Of course you are."

She grabbed her keys, her coat, and—after a brief, bitter hesitation—a pair of cotton gloves from the drawer. She didn't look at Nimbus when she said, "You're staying."

Nimbus hopped off the table and followed her anyway.

Clara didn't argue. That was the problem with living with a cat who talked. He didn't believe in permission.

The square was already buzzing when she drove through.

People stood in clusters outside the bakery, outside the hardware store, outside the post office—faces angled toward one another, mouths working with that awful town-language that wasn't quite sympathy and wasn't quite curiosity.

Clara kept her eyes on the road and her grip tight on the steering wheel.

A patrol car sat near the fountain at the center of town. Sheriff Halden's car, she realized, then corrected herself: not Halden's. The county's. They never let it feel like it belonged to one man.

She parked behind her shop and entered through the back door.

Nimbus trotted in after her, tail up like he owned the place.

Clara went straight to the cabinet under the counter. Her fingers trembled as she unlocked it.

The wooden box sat where she'd left it.

She pulled it out, set it on the counter, and stared at it for a full five seconds before lifting the lid.

The pocket watch waited in its faded velvet cradle, silver and calm.

Clara put on the gloves.

Nimbus hopped onto the counter and planted himself between her and the watch, eyes narrow. "Slow."

"I'm being slow," Clara muttered.

"Slower."

Clara exhaled and reached in. The moment her gloved fingers touched the metal, a shiver of sensation ran up her arm—not as violent as yesterday, but sharp enough to make her teeth clench.

Darkness.

Pressure.

A gasp that wasn't hers.

And underneath it, something new this time—something she hadn't caught through the panic.

A *presence*.

Not a ghost. Not a voice. Just the undeniable awareness that someone else had been close, close enough for breath.

Clara swallowed and forced herself to stay in the moment. She turned the watch over in her hands, examining it as if she were only an appraiser.

The casing was scratched. Not the gentle wear of decades, but new lines, jagged and hurried. Like it had been scraped against stone or metal.

Her pulse sped up.

"Clara," Nimbus said softly.

"I know." Her voice shook. "This isn't—this isn't a fall."

Nimbus's ears flattened. "Say it again. Out loud. So you stop trying to convince yourself otherwise."

Clara swallowed. "Travis didn't just fall."

Nimbus nodded once, satisfied.

Clara turned the watch and pressed her gloved thumb along the hinge until the casing popped open.

The face was old, cream-colored, marked with fine cracks like a dried riverbed. Roman numerals. A second hand frozen at a strange angle.

The time read **4:17**.

Clara's stomach tightened.

"Is that when it happened?" she whispered.

Nimbus's gaze flicked to her face. "Could be when it stopped. Could be when he stopped."

Clara forced a breath and reached carefully for the winding crown. She didn't want to trigger anything else, but she needed to know if the watch was broken or simply unwound.

The second she touched the crown, the echo slammed into her again—harder than before. Not the same panic, but the moment *after*.

A breathless hush.

A heartbeat pounding in someone's ears.

A thought, sharp and frantic:

Don't tell. Don't tell. Don't tell.

Clara's hands jerked. The watch snapped shut with a metallic click.

She sucked in air like she'd surfaced from deep water.

Nimbus's paw landed on her wrist—light pressure, grounding. "Enough."

Clara's eyes burned. "Someone was with him."

Nimbus's voice was flat. "Yes."

"And they didn't want anyone to know."

Nimbus didn't blink. "Also yes."

Clara stared down at the watch. Its weight felt heavier now, like it had turned into evidence.

If she went to the sheriff with this, what would she say?

Hello, Sheriff, I touched a watch and it told me a man died?

Even in Briar Hollow, people had limits.

Clara leaned over the counter and rubbed her forehead, gloves still on. "I can't—"

Nimbus's voice cut in. "You can."

Clara looked at him, incredulous. "No. I can't. I'm not a cop. I'm not even—" She stopped herself before she said *normal*.

Nimbus's tail swished. "You don't have to be a cop to ask questions."

Clara's phone buzzed on the counter. A text from an unknown number.

Sheriff Halden: I heard you had Travis Rowe's watch in your shop. Call me.

Clara stared at the screen until the words blurred.

Nimbus leaned closer, reading over her shoulder like he could. "Well," he said. "That's inconvenient."

Clara's throat tightened. "How does he know?"

Nimbus's eyes narrowed. "Because small towns don't keep secrets."

Clara felt the echo again, faint now, like a cold hand on the back of her neck.

Don't tell.

She stared at the sheriff's message.

Then she typed back with fingers that didn't feel like hers.

Clara: I can come by.

Nimbus's ears twitched. "You just volunteered."

"I know."

Nimbus hopped down from the counter. "Then we'd better rehearse your lies."

Clara gave him a sharp look. "I'm not lying."

Nimbus's yellow eyes gleamed. "Then you're going to be very careful with the truth."

Clara closed the box, locked it back in the cabinet, and slid the key into her pocket.

Outside, the town buzzed with grief and gossip.

Inside, Clara stood behind her counter, heart pounding, knowing one thing with absolute clarity:

Travis Rowe was dead.

And the quarry wasn't the one keeping the secret.

Chapter Three

What the Sheriff Notices

The Briar Hollow Sheriff's Office sat one block off the square, tucked behind a line of dogwoods that did nothing to make it less intimidating.

Clara parked, sat for a moment with her hands on the steering wheel, and told her heart to calm down.

It did not listen.

Nimbus remained in the passenger seat, watching the building like it might lunge. "Remember," he said, "you're a concerned shop owner, not a woman with a screaming watch."

Clara swallowed. "I know."

"You say that," Nimbus replied, "but you have a terrible track record with secrets."

Clara ignored him, grabbed her coat, and got out of the car. She locked the door out of habit—then paused, looked at Nimbus through the window, and unlocked it again.

"Stay," she said firmly.

Nimbus blinked. "I'm not welcome in government buildings."

"You're not welcome anywhere," Clara said. "But you're staying."

Nimbus sniffed. "I'll judge you from here."

She took that as agreement.

Inside, the station smelled like ham sandwiches, paper, and old heating vents. A deputy she didn't recognize looked up from the desk.

"Clara Finch," he said, already knowing. "Sheriff's expecting you."

Of course he was.

Sheriff Halden's office door stood open. He sat behind his desk, sleeves rolled up, glasses perched low on his nose as he studied a folder thick with paper.

He looked up when Clara stepped inside.

"Clara," he said, tone easy. "Appreciate you coming in."

She closed the door behind her. "You said you wanted to talk."

He gestured to the chair across from him. "I did."

Clara sat, folding her hands in her lap so he wouldn't see how tightly her fingers were clenched.

Halden didn't rush. He finished reading a page, slid it into the folder, and finally met her eyes.

"Travis Rowe," he said. "You knew him?"

"Yes." Clara chose the word carefully. "As much as anyone does in Briar Hollow."

Halden huffed softly. "Fair." He leaned back. "You had his watch."

Clara nodded. "His sister brought it in yesterday for appraisal."

"And you kept it."

"I do that sometimes," Clara said. "For research."

Halden's gaze stayed on her face, sharp but not hostile. "You have any idea why he'd give you something like that?"

Clara hesitated just long enough to be honest without being reckless. "He trusted me."

Halden's eyebrow lifted. "Trusted you with what?"

She met his eyes. "His property."

Halden studied her for a moment, then nodded as if that answer fit somewhere into a puzzle he'd already started assembling.

"Walk me through yesterday," he said.

Clara did. Carefully. The shop. Vesta. The box. The watch. She left out the echo. Left out the panic. Left out the part where the object screamed like it had a mouth.

When she finished, Halden leaned forward, forearms on the desk.

"You drop things often?" he asked.

Clara's stomach tightened. "What?"

"The watch," he said. "Vesta said you dropped it."

Clara forced a small smile. "I was distracted."

Halden didn't smile back. "By what?"

She held his gaze. "By the fact that her brother was missing."

A beat passed.

Then Halden nodded slowly. "Reasonable."

Clara let out a breath she hadn't realized she'd been holding.

Halden tapped the folder. "We ruled the death an accident pending autopsy. Quarry's steep. Ground's unstable. Happens more than folks like to think."

Clara's pulse ticked up. "Pending?"

Halden's eyes flicked to her. "Meaning not final."

She swallowed. "Then why are people already saying it's closed?"

"Because people like certainty," Halden said. "Even when it's wrong."

Clara's heart stuttered.

Halden continued, casual now. "You notice anything unusual about the watch?"

Clara chose her words like stepping stones. "It's damaged."

"How?"

"Scratches," she said. "Recent. Not wear."

Halden nodded once, as if he'd expected that. "Anything else?"

Clara hesitated.

Nimbus's voice echoed in her head. *Careful with the truth.*

"The time," she said finally. "It stopped."

Halden's gaze sharpened. "At?"

"Four seventeen," Clara said. "That could mean anything. Or nothing."

Halden studied her for a long moment, then flipped open the folder and slid a photo across the desk.

It showed the quarry's edge. Yellow tape. A blur of uniforms.

A timestamp glowed in the corner of the image.

4:19 PM.

Clara's breath caught.

Halden watched her reaction closely. "That's when the call came in."

Her fingers curled against her palm.

"That's close," she said carefully.

Halden leaned back. "Close enough to make me curious."

Clara forced herself to meet his eyes. "Curious about what?"

"About why a man who supposedly slipped managed to keep his watch intact," Halden said, "but scratched the casing like he was dragging it across stone."

Clara's mouth went dry.

Halden sighed and removed his glasses, rubbing the bridge of his nose. "Look, Clara. I'm not accusing you of anything. I'm asking because you're observant. Because you notice details other people don't."

Clara's heart hammered.

"And," Halden added quietly, "because Travis Rowe was not alone yesterday."

Her pulse spiked. "You know that?"

Halden shook his head. "I suspect it."

Clara's chest tightened. "Then why call it an accident?"

"Because suspicion isn't proof," Halden said. "And proof takes time."

He leaned forward again. "You hear anything around town? See anything strange come through your shop?"

Clara thought of the watch. Of the panic. Of the thought that wasn't words.

Don't tell.

She chose a different truth.

"People are scared," she said. "They don't want trouble tied to the quarry."

Halden nodded. "There it is."

He closed the folder. "Officially, I'd appreciate it if you didn't interfere."

Clara swallowed. "And unofficially?"

Halden held her gaze, expression unreadable. "Unofficially, if you notice anything relevant... I won't ask how you noticed."

Clara's breath left her in a rush.

Halden stood. "Bring me the watch tomorrow."

Clara rose slowly. "Tomorrow?"

"I want it logged." He paused. "After you finish your appraisal."

Clara nodded. "All right."

As she turned toward the door, Halden spoke again.

"Clara."

She looked back.

He met her eyes steadily. "Be careful."

She didn't trust her voice, so she just nodded and left.

Nimbus was sitting on the hood of her car when she stepped outside.

"You took too long," he said.

Clara unlocked the door and slid into the driver's seat. "He knows."

Nimbus hopped down and climbed inside. "He suspects."

"He showed me the time."

Nimbus's ears angled forward. "Good. That means you're not crazy."

Clara started the engine with shaking hands. "He wants the watch tomorrow."

Nimbus's tail flicked. "Then today is your window."

Clara pulled out of the lot, the station shrinking in her rearview mirror.

"Today for what?" she asked.

Nimbus's eyes gleamed. "To find out who was with Travis Rowe before the quarry took the blame."

Clara's stomach tightened, but beneath it, something steadied.

The town might want this quiet.

She didn't.

And neither did the watch.

Chapter Four

Scratches on Stone

C lara drove past the square without stopping.

It wasn't avoidance—it was instinct. The town was too loud right now, buzzing with certainty it hadn't earned. She needed quieter places. Places where people talked without realizing they were doing it.

Nimbus watched the familiar streets slide past. "You're heading toward the quarry road."

"I'm heading toward the *people* near the quarry road," Clara said. "There's a difference."

"Splitting hairs," Nimbus replied. "The quarry wins either way."

She pulled into the gravel lot beside Henson's Hardware instead, the old bell on the door jingling as she stepped inside. The place smelled like oil, rubber, and sawdust—a scent that felt stubbornly unchanged no matter how many decades passed.

If anyone knew who had business near the quarry, it was Cal Henson.

Cal stood behind the counter, broad-shouldered and graying, flipping through invoices with the intense focus of a man who pretended numbers didn't scare him. He looked up and smiled when he saw her.

"Clara Finch," he said. "You here for nails or answers?"

Clara managed a thin smile. "Depends what you've got in stock."

Nimbus muttered, "Ask him before he remembers he doesn't like you."

Cal leaned on the counter. "I heard about Travis."

Clara nodded. "Everyone has."

Cal grimaced. "Hard man to like. Harder to lose."

Clara chose her angle carefully. "He'd been asking around about quarry access lately, hadn't he?"

Cal's eyebrows lifted. "That's a specific question."

Clara shrugged. "I run an antique shop. I notice things."

Nimbus snorted quietly.

Cal hesitated, then sighed. "Yeah. He came in last week. Wanted climbing rope. Said he needed it for 'inspection work.'"

Clara's pulse ticked up. "Inspection of what?"

Cal shook his head. "Didn't say. Wouldn't say. Paid cash."

Nimbus's ears twitched. "Paid cash is never comforting."

"Did he mention anyone else?" Clara asked.

Cal rubbed his jaw. "He asked about land surveys. Old boundary markers. The kind that get lost when towns stop caring."

Clara's stomach tightened. "Did you point him anywhere?"

Cal nodded reluctantly. "I told him to talk to Evan Pike. Evan's been contracted by the county for environmental assessments."

Nimbus stiffened. "There it is."

Clara kept her voice neutral. "Evan Pike?"

Cal snorted. "Quiet guy. Knows his paperwork. Keeps his head down."

Clara thanked Cal, bought a box of gloves she didn't need to justify the visit, and stepped back outside.

She sat in the car for a moment, hands on the wheel.

"Suspect number one," Nimbus said. "Too neat."

"I agree," Clara said. "Which makes me nervous."

She drove toward the county offices on the edge of town, the building squat and beige, designed to discourage lingering. Evan Pike's name was listed on the directory under *Environmental & Land Use*.

The receptionist eyed Clara warily but waved her through.

Evan Pike was younger than Clara expected. Early thirties. Thin. Neatly dressed. He looked up from his computer when she knocked, surprise flashing across his face.

"Clara Finch," he said. "Antiques, right?"

"Second Chances," she replied. "I won't take much of your time."

Nimbus settled himself on the windowsill, tail wrapped tight. "Liar."

Evan gestured to the chair. "What can I help you with?"

Clara didn't sit. "Travis Rowe came to see you recently."

Evan's jaw tightened almost imperceptibly. "Yes."

"About the quarry."

"Yes."

"Why?"

Evan folded his hands on the desk. "That's not really public—"

"He's dead," Clara said quietly.

The words changed the room.

Evan swallowed. "I know."

Clara studied him—not his face, but the objects around him. The pen on his desk. The clipboard leaning against the wall. The folded map tucked half under a stack of files.

Nimbus's voice dropped. "That map is screaming."

Clara slipped on her gloves.

Evan noticed. His eyes narrowed. "What are you doing?"

"Being careful," Clara said.

She reached for the map.

The echo rolled through her—not panic this time, but tension. Tight, coiled urgency. Arguments without shouting. Words sharpened by restraint.

You don't understand what this means.

Her breath caught.

Evan pushed back from his desk. "You can't just—"

Clara lifted her head. "You argued with Travis."

Evan's mouth tightened. "Everyone argued with Travis."

"About the quarry," she pressed.

Silence stretched.

Nimbus watched Evan like a hawk.

Finally, Evan exhaled. "He found something. Old documentation that suggested part of the quarry land was misclassified. If it went public, development would stall for years."

"Who benefits from development?" Clara asked.

Evan's eyes flicked away. "Investors. The town council. Anyone who wants jobs."

Clara's heart thudded. "And you?"

Evan met her gaze sharply. "I benefit from doing my job."

Nimbus scoffed. "And I benefit from naps."

Clara lowered the map. "Did you meet him yesterday?"

Evan shook his head too quickly. "No."

Clara studied the echo again—the urgency, the restraint. Not fear. Not guilt.

She nodded slowly. "All right."

Evan blinked. "That's it?"

"For now," Clara said. "One more thing—did Travis mention anyone else?"

Evan hesitated. "He said he was meeting someone after he left my office. Someone who 'needed convincing.'"

"Did he say who?"

Evan shook his head. "No."

Clara thanked him and left.

Back in the car, Nimbus exhaled. "He's hiding something, but not murder."

"That's what I felt," Clara said. "He's our false lead."

Nimbus's eyes gleamed. "Which means the real one is quieter."

Clara pulled away from the curb.

Her phone buzzed again.

A text from Sheriff Halden.

Halden: Autopsy moved up. I'll have preliminary findings tonight.

Clara's grip tightened on the wheel.

Nimbus leaned forward. "And there it is."

Clara stared at the road ahead, heart pounding.

The scratches on the watch hadn't come from a fall.

And Evan Pike hadn't pushed anyone.

Which meant the person who had was still walking around Briar Hollow, listening to everyone say *accident* and believing—wrongly—that silence would protect them.

Clara exhaled slowly.

It wouldn't.

Chapter Five

What Silence Sounds Like

C lara didn't go home.

She told herself it was because she needed groceries, because her fridge held nothing but mustard and good intentions—but that was a lie she didn't bother polishing. Home meant thinking. Thinking meant replaying echoes she couldn't afford to soften.

Instead, she drove the long way around town, past the old mill road and the sagging fence that pretended to keep people out of the quarry access trail. Sheriff Halden had said accident. The town had agreed. But the watch had said *don't tell*, and that was louder than gossip.

Nimbus watched the trees blur past. "You're circling."

"I'm narrowing," Clara said.

"Same shape," Nimbus replied.

She pulled into the gravel lot of the Briar Hollow Diner just before dusk. The place glowed like a promise—yellow light, steam-fogged windows, the low murmur of voices pretending nothing had shifted.

If anyone knew what Travis Rowe had been doing yesterday afternoon, it would be here.

Inside, the bell over the door chimed and the familiar smell of frying oil and burgers wrapped around her. A few heads turned. A few didn't. Grief had already settled into routine.

"Hey, Clara," called June from behind the counter. "Usual?"

Clara nodded. "To go."

Nimbus hopped onto the empty stool beside her, ignoring the look June shot him. "I'm invisible," he murmured. "Like consequences."

June slid a paper bag across the counter. "Rough day."

Clara hesitated. "Did Travis come in yesterday?"

June's hands stilled. Just for a second. "Yeah. Late lunch. Real late."

"Anyone with him?"

June shook her head. "No. But he wasn't alone."

Clara's pulse quickened. "What do you mean?"

June leaned in slightly, lowering her voice. "He kept looking at the door. Like he was waiting for someone. Or didn't want someone to walk in."

Nimbus's ears angled forward. "That's not a man planning to fall."

"What time?" Clara asked.

June frowned, thinking. "Little after four. I remember because the fryer timer went off and scared the life out of him."

Clara's throat tightened. "Did he leave alone?"

"Yes. Paid fast. Didn't touch his pie."

That landed harder than it should have.

Clara thanked June and stepped back outside, the sky bruising purple over the hills.

In the car, Nimbus was quiet longer than usual.

"What?" Clara asked.

Nimbus's tail flicked. "You're going to hate this part."

Clara started the engine. "I already do."

Nimbus met her eyes. "The echo on the watch wasn't rage. It wasn't panic alone either. It was *hesitation*."

Clara swallowed. "Say more."

"Whoever was with Travis didn't come to hurt him," Nimbus said. "They came to stop him from saying something."

Clara's hands tightened on the wheel. "Silence."

Nimbus nodded. "And silence doesn't always mean murder. Sometimes it means a shove, a bad angle, and a moment where someone decides not to reach out."

The quarry road curved ahead, darkening fast.

Clara didn't turn toward it.

She turned toward the Rowe house.

Vesta answered the door with red eyes and rigid posture, like she was holding herself together with habit alone.

"Clara," she said flatly. "If you're here to tell me it was an accident—"

"I'm not," Clara said.

Vesta's breath hitched. She stepped aside without a word.

Inside, the house smelled like lemon cleaner and grief. The kind that lingered even after people left.

Clara didn't sit. She didn't soften her voice.

"Did Travis mention anyone by name recently?" she asked.

Vesta's jaw worked. "He said someone was trying to rush the quarry sale through. Someone who 'owed him.'"

"Who?"

Vesta hesitated. "Councilwoman Reed."

Clara's stomach dropped.

Nimbus's voice was sharp. "That's your quiet."

"She and Travis went back years," Vesta continued. "Old deal. Old favor. He said if he talked, it would ruin her."

Clara felt the echo align in her chest like tumblers in a lock.

Don't tell.

Vesta looked at her, eyes suddenly fierce. "You think she did this."

"I think she was there," Clara said carefully. "I think Travis threatened to expose something. I think she panicked."

Vesta's shoulders sagged. "And pushed him."

Clara didn't answer.

She didn't need to.

Outside, night settled over Briar Hollow, and somewhere beyond the trees, the quarry waited—silent, patient, falsely blamed.

Clara stepped back onto the porch, heart pounding.

Nimbus exhaled. "Now you're dangerous."

Clara nodded once.

Because now she knew what silence sounded like.

And it wasn't empty at all.

Chapter Six

What Gets Written Down

C lara slept for exactly three hours.

Not because she was tired—because her body eventually overruled her mind and shut the lights off whether she agreed or not. When she woke, the certainty was still there, solid and unwelcome, like a stone behind her ribs.

Councilwoman Reed.

Not a villain. Not a mastermind. A woman who'd made a decision years ago and spent every day since making sure it stayed buried.

Nimbus sat on the dresser, tail wrapped tight, watching Clara pull on clean clothes with the focus of someone preparing for weather rather than weathering consequences.

"You're going to the station," he said.

"Yes."

"You're going to say very little."

"Yes."

Nimbus narrowed his eyes. "That was too easy."

Clara slipped the cabinet key into her pocket. "I'm not accusing anyone. I'm giving the sheriff something he can verify."

Nimbus hopped down. "Paper beats panic."

Sheriff Halden's office smelled sharper this morning—cleaner, like someone had tried to scrub the uncertainty out of the walls.

Halden looked up when Clara entered, expression unreadable. "You're early."

"I didn't sleep," Clara said.

He nodded like that tracked. "Autopsy's preliminary is back."

Her pulse thudded. "And?"

"No clear signs of a fight," Halden said. "But the angle's wrong for a simple fall. Impact points don't line up."

Clara exhaled slowly. "So not an accident."

"Not yet," Halden said. "But not clean either."

She set the wooden box on his desk. "I brought the watch."

He opened it carefully, gloved hands respectful. "You notice anything else?"

Clara kept her voice steady. "The scratches are consistent with stone, not ground. And the time stopped within minutes of the emergency call."

Halden studied the watch, then her. "You're sure about the scratches?"

"I am."

He nodded once and slid the box aside. "You want to tell me how you know?"

Clara met his gaze. "I look closely."

A beat passed.

Halden didn't push.

Instead, he opened a different folder and slid a document across the desk.

A zoning amendment. Quarry land. Fast-tracked approval.

Signed by **Councilwoman Elaine Reed**.

Clara's chest tightened. "That went through last month."

"Quietly," Halden said. "Against staff recommendation."

Clara nodded. "Travis knew."

Halden's jaw tightened. "He requested records two days ago."

"And yesterday," Clara said softly, "he met with her."

Halden's eyes sharpened. "You have proof?"

"Not yet," Clara said. "But she had motive. And opportunity."

Halden leaned back, weighing it. "That's not enough to bring her in."

"I know," Clara said. "But it's enough to listen."

Halden studied her for a long moment. Then he stood.

"Stay here," he said.

He returned ten minutes later with a second folder and a look that confirmed her instincts hadn't been wrong.

"Councilwoman Reed says she didn't see Travis yesterday," Halden said. "Says she was in meetings all afternoon."

Clara's voice stayed calm. "With witnesses?"

"Two," Halden said. "Both city employees."

Nimbus's voice echoed in her head. *Paper lies when people agree.*

Clara took a breath. "Sheriff... did anyone check her phone records?"

Halden's eyes narrowed. "Why?"

"Because Travis was at the diner at four," Clara said. "He was waiting for someone. And the watch stopped at four seventeen."

Halden was already reaching for the phone.

An hour later, Clara stood in the hallway while Halden made the call.

Councilwoman Reed arrived twenty minutes after that—composed, professional, and visibly irritated.

She didn't look like a killer.

She looked like someone who believed the story would hold.

Halden laid out the timeline calmly. The diner. The quarry access. The zoning vote.

Reed corrected him once.

Just once.

"Travis left at four fifteen," she said sharply. "I watched him go."

The room went very still.

Halden looked at her. "You watched him?"

Reed froze.

Clara felt the echo in her chest without touching a thing—panic this time, sharp and unmistakable.

Reed's composure cracked. "I—I meant I assumed—"

Halden closed the folder. "Councilwoman, we need you to come with us."

Her shoulders sagged, the truth collapsing under its own weight.

"It wasn't supposed to happen," Reed whispered. "I just needed him to stop talking. He stepped back. He slipped. I didn't push him—I just didn't grab him."

Silence filled the room.

Halden's voice was steady. "That's for the court to decide."

As they led her away, Clara finally let out the breath she'd been holding since yesterday morning.

Nimbus's voice was quiet now. "That's what silence sounds like."

Clara nodded.

Outside, Briar Hollow went on pretending.

Inside, the truth had been written down.

And this time, it wouldn't stay buried.

Chapter Seven

When the Echo Lets Go

B riar Hollow absorbed the news the way it absorbed everything else—slowly, unevenly, and with a noticeable lack of apology.

By midmorning, the sheriff's cars were gone from the square, replaced by speculation. Councilwoman Reed's name moved through town in hushed tones, growing heavier with each repetition. Some people sounded shocked. Others sounded relieved. A few sounded offended, as if the truth had personally inconvenienced them.

Clara didn't stay to listen.

She unlocked *Second Chances Antiques* and stepped inside, the familiar hush settling around her like a held breath finally released. The shop felt different today. Lighter. As if something lodged in its walls had worked itself free overnight.

Nimbus hopped onto the counter and surveyed the room. "Well," he said, "we've officially made ourselves unpopular with at least three powerful people."

Clara set her purse down and exhaled. "That's a record low."

Nimbus sniffed. "Give it time."

She went straight to the cabinet under the counter and unlocked it. The wooden box waited where she'd left it, obedient and quiet.

Clara hesitated before opening it.

For the first time since Vesta had placed it on the counter, she wasn't afraid of what she'd feel.

She lifted the lid.

The pocket watch lay in its velvet cradle, silver dulled by age and handling. Ordinary now. Heavy, yes—but no longer loud.

Clara slipped on her gloves and picked it up.

Nothing rushed at her.

No panic. No pressure. No breathless command to keep silent.

Just the faint residue of grief—soft, human, and bearable.

Clara swallowed past the lump in her throat.

Nimbus watched closely. "Gone?"

She nodded. "Gone."

Nimbus relaxed, just a fraction. "Good. I hate it when they linger."

The bell over the door chimed.

Vesta Rowe stepped inside, looking like she hadn't slept and didn't intend to. Her eyes went straight to Clara's face.

"It's true," Vesta said. "They arrested her."

Clara nodded. "Yes."

Vesta stood there for a long moment, shoulders trembling—not with rage this time, but release. "He wasn't crazy," she whispered. "He wasn't careless."

"No," Clara said gently. "He wasn't."

Vesta crossed the room and stopped at the counter, gaze dropping to the open box. "Is it... is it finished?"

Clara held the watch up carefully. "It's quiet."

Vesta pressed a hand to her mouth. Tears spilled freely now, unguarded. "Thank you."

Clara shook her head. "I didn't do this alone."

Vesta gave a brittle laugh. "In this town? Nobody ever does."

She took the watch with reverent hands. For the first time, Clara didn't flinch when she passed it over.

Vesta closed the box. "Travis would've liked knowing it mattered."

"It did," Clara said.

Vesta hesitated at the door. "You're going to get a reputation for this."

Clara smiled faintly. "I already have one."

Vesta nodded once and left.

The shop settled back into silence.

Nimbus stretched luxuriously. "Well. Murder solved. Town rattled. Ego bruised."

Clara leaned against the counter, suddenly exhausted. "And?"

Nimbus looked at her. "And you're still here. That's the important part."

Clara closed her eyes.

She hadn't planned to be involved. She hadn't wanted to be noticed. But the echoes didn't care what she wanted—and neither, apparently, did Briar Hollow.

She straightened, flipped the sign to *Open*, and took a steadying breath.

Nimbus smirked. "You know someone else is going to bring you something soon."

Clara glanced at the door. "I know."

Nimbus's tail curled. "Different object. Different silence."

Clara nodded.

Because some stories ended.

And some—quietly, insistently—knocked again.

Quiet Profits in Briar Hollow

The Quiet Discretion Mysteries - Book Two

Petra Shaw

CSD Digital Enterprises, LLC

Chapter One

Hush Money in Briar Hollow

The ledger smelled like old leather and dust.

Clara Whitlock noticed that before she noticed the woman holding it.

The bell over the door chimed just after lunch, a careful, apologetic sound that matched the posture of the woman stepping into *Second Chances Antiques*. She hesitated on the threshold as if the shop itself might object to her presence, then crossed the floor with slow, deliberate steps, a canvas tote clutched tightly to her chest.

Nimbus lifted his head from his post in the front window. His yellow eyes narrowed to sharp slits.

"Oh," he said quietly. "That's not a cookbook."

Clara didn't reach for the tote. She didn't even smile yet. Experience had taught her that certain objects—and the people who carried them—needed acknowledgment before contact. Rushing either usually ended poorly.

"Hi," the woman said. Her voice carried the faint strain of someone who'd rehearsed the moment and still hadn't settled on the right tone. "I was told you might be able to tell me if this is... anything."

Clara nodded and gestured to the counter. "Why don't you start by telling me where it came from."

The woman hesitated, then set the tote down as if it were heavier than it looked. "My uncle's house. He passed last week. Heart, they said." She made a vague motion with her hand, as if hearts were faulty appliances rather than organs. "I'm clearing things out. There's... a lot."

"I'm sorry," Clara said, and meant it.

The woman shrugged, but the motion didn't reach her eyes. "He was complicated."

Nimbus snorted. "They always are."

Clara shot him a warning look and reached for her gloves—thin cotton, folded neatly beneath the counter. Habit now. Professionalism. Or fear that had learned to behave itself.

When she opened the tote, the ledger sat right on top.

No attempt to hide it. No careful wrapping. Just a battered leather book with a cracked spine and softened corners, the kind of thing that had been handled often and intentionally. A bent clasp hung loose at the side, its hinge worn thin, as if someone had worried it open and shut more times than they cared to admit.

Clara didn't touch it yet.

The feeling pressed in anyway.

Not panic. Not grief. Just tightness.

Counting.

A controlled, persistent tally, like fingers tapping against a tabletop while someone waited for a confirmation that never quite arrived.

Clara kept her breathing slow and even. "Did you ever see him use this?"

The woman shook her head. "No. He kept it in a drawer. Locked." Her brow furrowed. "Which is strange. He didn't lock anything else."

Nimbus hopped onto the counter and leaned closer, nose twitching. "Locked drawers are where people keep the parts of themselves they don't want audited."

Clara slipped on her gloves and lifted the ledger.

The echo sharpened immediately.

Anxiety—controlled, practiced. Numbers lining up with mechanical precision. Relief, brief and almost pleasant. Then something threaded through it all, thin but unmistakable.

Fear.

Clara's jaw tightened.

She opened the ledger.

The pages were yellowed but meticulously neat, the handwriting precise to the point of obsession. Dates marched down the left margin. Amounts stood to attention on the right. Short notes filled the narrow space between them.

Consulting.

Permit assistance.

Fee.

Nothing illegal at first glance. Nothing dramatic. Language designed to survive scrutiny.

But the rhythm was wrong.

Too regular. Too careful. Too consistent to be casual.

Nimbus leaned in. "That's not spending."

Clara turned a page. Then another. "It's maintenance."

Initials repeated across the paper. Sometimes three letters. Sometimes two. Occasionally just one. Familiar shapes without names attached.

"Do these mean anything to you?" Clara asked, keeping her tone neutral.

The woman leaned forward, squinting. "No. I never saw this before."

Clara closed the book gently. "I'll need some time to research it."

The woman exhaled with visible relief. "That's fine. If it's nothing, you can toss it."

Nimbus's gaze snapped up. "People never say that unless they're hoping you won't."

Clara met the woman's eyes steadily. "I won't toss it."

The woman swallowed, nodded once, and left quickly—too quickly—like someone relieved to be done with the asking.

When the door closed, the shop felt quieter than before.

Nimbus stretched. "So. Who's been paying whom to sleep at night?"

Clara traced one gloved finger along the ledger's edge. "Someone who thought this solved a problem."

Nimbus's tail flicked. "And then stopped."

Clara's phone buzzed on the counter.

The display said: **June (Diner):** You hear about Carl Benton?

Clara's stomach dipped.

Carl Benton owned half the commercial properties on the south end of town. He sponsored parades, cut ribbons, and smiled like nothing ever cost him anything.

She typed back.

Clara: No. What happened?

The dots appeared. Disappeared. Appeared again.

June: Found him this morning. In his recliner. Looked peaceful.

Clara closed her eyes.

Nimbus didn't speak.

Clara set the ledger down, the neat rows of numbers suddenly heavier than paper had any right to be.

Peaceful deaths didn't usually arrive with ledgers full of quiet payments.

She locked the book in the cabinet beneath the counter and slid the key into her pocket, the familiar weight grounding her.

Nimbus watched her carefully. "Tell me you're not thinking what I think you're thinking."

Clara met his gaze. "Someone just lost their income."

Nimbus sighed. "And now they're motivated."

Outside, Briar Hollow carried on with its afternoon errands, already practicing the word *natural* in lowered voices.

Inside, Clara stood very still, listening to the silence the ledger left behind.

It wasn't empty.
It was keeping count.

Chapter Two

Amounts Owed

B riar Hollow had a way of turning death into punctuation.

   A pause.

A lowered voice.

A casserole wrapped in foil and expectation.

   Carl Benton's death earned all three before sunset.

   By the time Clara unlocked *Second Chances Antiques* the next morning, the town had already decided what kind of story it wanted.

   Peaceful. Natural. Sad, but not disruptive.

   Those words floated through the square like fallen leaves—light enough to drift anywhere, heavy enough to cover what people didn't want to see underneath.

   Clara heard Carl's name twice before she even turned the sign to *Open*. Once from a woman walking a golden retriever who slowed as she passed the shop window. Once from an older man buying picture frames who said it in the careful, even tone reserved for weather updates.

   "Peaceful, they say," the man added, as if peace were a favor Carl Benton had finally done the town.

Clara nodded, rang him up, and locked the door behind him with a little more force than necessary.

Nimbus hopped onto the counter and flicked his tail like a metronome keeping time with Clara's irritation. "I hate that word."

"Which one?" Clara asked, even though she knew.

"Peaceful," Nimbus said. "It's what people say when they don't want to ask follow-up questions."

Clara pressed her palms flat on the counter and breathed in slowly—wood polish, old paper, lemon oil. Familiar scents. Safe scents. Her shop did not usually smell like rumors. This week, it did.

"That's how Briar Hollow survives," Clara said.

Nimbus blinked, unimpressed. "That's how Briar Hollow avoids accountability."

Clara didn't argue, because Nimbus was irritatingly correct more often than was healthy.

Her phone rang.

She didn't need to look at the screen to guess. Halden never called to chat, and no one else had the sense to call before nine.

"Clara Whitlock," she answered.

"Clara." Sheriff Halden's voice was level, familiar, and faintly tired. "You hear about Benton?"

"Yes."

"Good. Saves me some explaining." Paper rustled on his end, like he was already building the official version in a file folder. "Natural causes, most likely. He had a known heart condition."

Clara leaned her hip against the counter, gaze drifting—without meaning to—to the cabinet beneath it. "Most likely."

There was a small pause. Not a reaction. Just the quiet recognition of a hesitation he chose not to name.

Halden didn't push. "You told me you'd flag anything odd."

"I did," Clara said carefully. "And I will."

Another pause. Longer this time.

"You sound tired," Halden said.

"I am."

"So am I," he replied, and the admission landed with more weight than the words themselves. "If you notice anything relevant—anything at all—you call me."

"I will," Clara said again.

They hung up without ceremony. No comfort. No warning. Just a line drawn between what could be said out loud and what couldn't.

Nimbus watched her set the phone down. "He's waiting."

"He's listening," Clara corrected.

Nimbus's ears twitched. "That's worse."

Clara turned the sign to *Open* out of habit. She lasted twelve minutes. One customer came in, browsed the glass case without seeing anything, and left without buying so much as a postcard. The town wasn't shopping today. It was processing. And processing in Briar Hollow meant talking in low voices, not spending money.

Clara flipped the sign to *Closed* again.

"Ah," Nimbus said. "The economy of grief."

Clara ignored him, knelt, and unlocked the cabinet.

The ledger waited exactly where she'd left it—silent, patient, smug in its neatness.

She set it on the counter and took a breath before opening it. The echo returned immediately. Less sharp than yesterday, but persistent: anxiety humming beneath the surface, numbers lining up, a relief that never lasted long enough to feel safe.

Clara flipped to the last page.

One entry stood alone.

C.B. — 3,000 — final

Her pulse ticked up.

Nimbus leaned forward. "Final," he read. "That's not a delay. That's a door slamming."

Clara traced the date with her gloved fingertip. Two weeks ago.

She flipped back a few pages.

The same initials.

The same amount.

Month after month, like clockwork.

"Three thousand dollars," Clara murmured. "Enough to matter. Not enough to draw attention."

Nimbus's tail flicked. "Comfort money."

"Silence money," Clara said.

She leaned closer, scanning the margins. Faint notes sat beside several entries—words written small enough to pretend they were nothing.

Delay.

Handled.

Hold.

Clara felt a chill settle between her shoulders.

"This wasn't bribery," she said slowly. "Not the loud kind. This was... maintenance."

Nimbus nodded. "Payments made to keep problems from becoming conversations."

Clara turned pages, careful and steady. The handwriting never changed. The rhythm never broke. Whoever kept this ledger had been consistent in the way only anxious people could be.

She flipped to the front.

There it was.

Not initials. Not coded.

Carl Benton — Primary

Her breath caught.

Nimbus stared at the page. "Primary payer."

"Yes," Clara said quietly. "Which means Carl wasn't being paid."

"He was paying," Nimbus finished. "And now he's dead."

Clara closed the ledger, the sound soft but final.

Outside, a car rolled past, its tires whispering on cold pavement. A dog barked once and fell silent. Life continued with its usual disinterest in human secrets.

Clara stared at the ledger as if it might explain itself.

"If someone killed Carl to keep this quiet," she said, "it wasn't because he was talking."

Nimbus hopped down from the counter and began pacing the length of the glass case, nails clicking softly like a countdown. "It's because he stopped."

Clara nodded, the conclusion settling like a stone.

She locked the ledger back in the cabinet and slid the key deeper into her pocket, as if distance could stop the implications from spreading.

She didn't go for her coat. She didn't turn the sign back to *Open*.

Instead, she stood behind the counter, listening to her shop and the town beyond it.

"Tomorrow," Nimbus said, voice dry, "you'll go ask questions."

Clara's mouth tightened. "Tomorrow I confirm what I already suspect."

Nimbus paused and looked at her. "And today?"

"Today," Clara said, "I stop pretending this is just bookkeeping."

Nimbus blinked slowly. "That's the spirit."

Clara turned off the lights she didn't need and looked once more at the cabinet under the counter.

The ledger didn't feel like a relic anymore.

It felt like a trigger.

Behind her, the shop settled into silence.
But the numbers in the ledger didn't rest.
They waited.

Chapter Three

What the Town Calls Peace

The pressure didn't arrive all at once.

It came in polite pieces.

Clara noticed it first at the post office.

She'd stopped in midmorning, more out of habit than necessity, and was standing in line behind Mrs. Calder when the woman turned, smiled too brightly, and said, "Such a shame about Carl."

Clara nodded. "It is."

Mrs. Calder leaned closer, lowering her voice as if grief itself were confidential. "But at least it was peaceful."

There it was again.

Peaceful.

Clara felt Nimbus's presence at her ankle, solid and warm. "That word is working overtime," he murmured.

Mrs. Calder continued, clearly relieved to have found a listener. "Carl did so much for this town. Jobs. Sponsorships. Donations. It would be awful if people started... questioning things."

Clara kept her expression neutral. "Questioning what?"

Mrs. Calder blinked, surprised. "Oh. You know. *Things.*" She laughed lightly, the sound brittle. "No sense dragging it out. That doesn't help anyone."

The clerk called Mrs. Calder forward, and the conversation dissolved as neatly as it had formed.

Nimbus looked up at Clara. "That wasn't concern."

"No," Clara said quietly. "That was instruction."

The second push came at the diner.

June slid Clara her usual mug—hot water, cinnamon stick—then hesitated instead of moving away.

"You stirring something up?" June asked, not unkindly.

Clara looked up. "Why would you ask that?"

June wiped the counter, already clean. "People are talking. Not loudly. But they're talking." She paused. "They don't like surprises."

Nimbus snorted. "They love secrets, though."

June glanced at the empty stool beside Clara and shivered. "Tell me you're being careful."

"I am," Clara said.

June nodded, not reassured. "Good. Because the word going around is *closure.*"

Clara frowned. "That's not a bad word."

"It is when it's being used as a lid," June said. "People want this done. Tidy. No loose ends."

Clara watched a man at the counter laugh a little too hard at nothing. "Loose ends make people nervous."

"They make people angry," June corrected.

Nimbus leaned closer to Clara's ear. "Anger wrapped in politeness is still anger."

By noon, the pressure had sharpened.

A woman browsing teacups asked, "You're not getting involved in all that unpleasantness, are you?"

A man buying a lamp said, "Best thing for Briar Hollow is to let things settle."

A delivery driver joked, "You've always had a knack for finding old junk. Just don't go digging up anything that should stay buried."

Each comment came with a smile.

Each smile carried the same message.

Stop.

Clara locked the shop early.

She stood behind the counter, hands braced against the wood, breathing through the weight of it. The town wasn't threatening her. It didn't need to.

It was reminding her where she lived.

Nimbus jumped onto the counter and paced. "They're afraid."

"Of what?" Clara asked.

"Of mirrors," Nimbus said. "Of losing the version of themselves where nothing ugly ever happened unless it was an accident."

Clara stared at the door. "They think I'm making it worse."

Nimbus stopped pacing. "They think you're making it visible."

That landed harder.

Clara exhaled slowly. "I didn't ask for this."

Nimbus flicked his tail. "Neither did Carl. But he's still dead."

A knock came at the door.

Not the bell.

A knock.

Clara froze.

Nimbus went utterly still.

"Clara?" called a familiar voice. "It's just me."

She recognized it—Tom Willis, head of the Chamber of Commerce. He stood outside smiling through the glass like a man practicing reassurance.

Clara unlocked the door but didn't invite him in.

Tom stepped just inside, hands raised slightly as if he were calming a skittish animal. "I won't take much of your time."

Nimbus muttered, "They never do."

Tom glanced around the shop. "You know, this place is such an asset to Briar Hollow. Quirky. Charming. People come here to feel comfortable."

Clara didn't respond.

Tom cleared his throat. "We've all had a rough couple of days. Emotions are high. Folks are just hoping things can return to normal."

"What's normal?" Clara asked.

Tom smiled wider. "Quiet."

There it was—said outright at last.

Clara met his gaze. "Quiet isn't the same as right."

Tom's smile tightened. "No one's asking you to do anything improper."

"Then what are you asking?" Clara said.

Tom hesitated, recalibrating. "Discretion."

Nimbus bared his teeth. "Ah. The polite word for silence."

Clara shook her head. "I don't sell discretion."

Tom's smile faltered. "Clara—"

"I sell objects," she said. "And sometimes the truth that clings to them."

A long beat passed.

Tom exhaled. "Just... be careful. Briar Hollow takes care of its own."

Clara watched him leave without replying.

When the door shut, the shop felt heavier than before.

Nimbus looked up at her. "That was the town asking nicely."

Clara nodded. "And if I say no?"

Nimbus's eyes gleamed. "Then they'll stop being nice."

Clara squared her shoulders.

"Then I won't be quiet," she said.

Nimbus smiled, sharp and proud. "Good. Neither will the ledger."

Chapter Four

Who Stops Getting Paid

Morning came sharp and bright, the kind of cold that made Briar Hollow look clean even when it was slightly untidy.

Frost webbed the edges of the shop windows, turning the glass into something between lace and warning. Clara unlocked the front door just after eight, and the bell chimed with its usual politeness—too cheerful for a town that had spent the last twenty-four hours practicing *natural causes* like it was a prayer.

She stepped inside and let the familiar smells wrap around her: cedar, lemon oil, old paper, faint dust warmed by yesterday's sun. The shop was quiet in the way it always was before customers arrived, but today that quiet felt tense—like the room was waiting for her to make a mistake.

Nimbus paused on the threshold with one paw lifted, head tilted, as if he could read the mood in the air.

"It still smells like money," he said. "And not the good kind."

Clara hung her coat on the hook. "There is no good kind."

Nimbus blinked slowly. "You say that, and yet you keep accepting it from strangers."

Clara ignored him and went straight to the cabinet under the counter. She didn't let herself hesitate this time. Hesitation was how panic snuck in.

She unlocked the cabinet, pulled out the ledger, and set it on the counter where the morning light could hit it full-on. The cracked leather looked drier today. Less menacing. More like an exhausted animal that had carried too much weight for too long.

She opened to the front.

Carl Benton — Primary

The words sat there with infuriating calm.

Clara stared for three seconds—just long enough for the reality of it to settle again. Carl Benton, town benefactor and commercial landlord, had been paying someone. Regularly. Quietly. For years, if the thickness of the ledger meant what she thought it meant.

Nimbus hopped onto the counter and leaned over the page, whiskers twitching. "Let's be methodical," he said. "Who needed Carl alive?"

Clara flipped to the most recent pages. "People he paid."

"And who needed him quiet?" Nimbus asked, tone dry.

Clara didn't look up. "Probably the same people."

Nimbus's tail flicked once. "Which means the secret isn't the problem."

"The money is," Clara finished.

She pulled a notepad from under the counter and began copying initials. Four sets that repeated most often. She didn't try to decode them yet; she didn't have to. The pattern mattered more than the names at this stage.

She circled the last two weeks with a heavy pen stroke.

"Two weeks ago," she murmured, "everything changes."

Nimbus leaned closer. "That's when someone stopped getting paid."

"And panicked," Clara said.

She forced herself to slow down. Not because she wasn't sure, but because rushing made her sloppy—and sloppy was how people got hurt in small towns. She flipped back three months and checked again.

Same rhythm. Same amounts. Same careful language in the notes.

Then the sudden word: **final**.

Not delayed. Not reduced. Not renegotiated.

Stopped.

Clara tore the page from the notepad and folded it into quarters, tucking it into her coat pocket like a secret she could carry without letting it leak. She didn't trust leaving it on the counter, not with the shop's front door and its too-friendly bell between her and the world.

Nimbus tracked her movement. "Where are we going?"

"The diner," Clara said.

Nimbus's ears perked. "Ah. Bacon truths."

Clara rolled her eyes. "People talk around food."

"They talk around coffee too," Nimbus said. "But you don't drink it, so we do bacon."

Clara grabbed her coat and locked the shop behind them.

The Briar Hollow Diner was already half-full. The air inside was warm and greasy in the comforting way only diners managed—fried potatoes, butter, sugar, and the steady drip of conversation that never truly stopped.

The bell on the diner door chimed as Clara stepped in, and she felt the tiniest shift in attention. Not a full turn of heads, but a slight quieting of voices. Carl Benton's name had turned the town into an animal listening for predators.

June spotted her immediately and poured a mug without asking. Clara didn't drink coffee, and June knew it, so she filled it with hot water and slid a small tin of cinnamon sticks along with it.

Clara's gratitude tightened her throat. "Thanks."

June leaned in, voice low. "You look like you're hunting."

Clara wrapped her hands around the warmth. "I have questions."

June snorted softly. "So does everyone. They just pretend they don't."

Clara kept her gaze on the counter, not on the customers. People didn't like being watched while they talked. "Did Carl change his routine lately?"

June's expression shifted—subtle, but real. "He stopped paying his tab."

Clara blinked. "Stopped?"

"Two weeks ago," June said. "Not like he couldn't afford it. Like he suddenly decided he didn't want to."

Nimbus, perched invisibly on the stool beside Clara, murmured, "That's your cut-off."

June continued, lowering her voice. "He paid cash that day—clean, exact amount, no tip—then said he was 'tightening things up.' After that, he didn't come in. Not once."

Clara's stomach tightened. "Carl Benton didn't miss breakfast."

June shook her head. "He missed nothing. He was a habit in a jacket. That's why it felt... wrong."

Clara nodded slowly. "Did he meet anyone here recently?"

June hesitated, then glanced toward the kitchen. When she looked back, her eyes were sharper. "Last Friday. Booth by the window."

"Who?" Clara asked.

June exhaled. "You didn't hear it from me."

Clara didn't rush her. She let the silence do its job.

Finally, June said, "Lydia Marsh. County permits. She comes in sometimes, always with a folder, always counting her cash twice before she pays. Nervous energy."

Nimbus went still. "That tracks."

Clara's pulse picked up. "What were they talking about?"

June leaned closer. "I only caught pieces. Carl said something like, 'I'm done paying for peace.' Lydia said, 'You can't just stop.'"

The words slid into place so neatly Clara almost hated them.

"Did Carl get angry?" Clara asked.

June shook her head. "No. He smiled. That's what bothered me. He had this... satisfied look. Like he'd finally decided something, and nobody could talk him out of it."

Clara's mind flashed to the word **final** in the ledger.

June watched her. "Clara... what are you doing?"

Clara didn't lie. She just didn't answer fully. "Making sure 'peaceful' means what they want it to mean."

June's face softened. "Be careful."

Clara left a few bills on the counter—more than the water was worth—and June pretended not to notice while still sliding them neatly into the tip jar like she didn't want the gesture to become a conversation.

Outside, the cold slapped Clara's cheeks awake again.

Nimbus padded beside her, tail low but purposeful. "Permit office," he said.

Clara nodded. "Permit office."

The County Permit Office was a squat brick building designed to discourage lingering. The lobby smelled like toner and old carpet, and the fluorescent lights were unforgiving in the way government buildings always were—bright enough to expose everything, warm enough to comfort nothing.

Clara signed in, waited, and listened to the bored rhythm of a wall clock that sounded too much like counting.

Lydia Marsh sat behind a desk stacked with folders. Her posture was rigid, her hair pulled back tight, glasses perched low on her nose. She looked up when Clara approached, surprise flickering across her face before it snapped into polite professionalism.

"Can I help you?" Lydia asked.

Clara smiled pleasantly, the way she did with difficult customers. "I hope so. I'm researching some old permits tied to Carl Benton."

Lydia's fingers paused over the keyboard.

"I'm not sure why that would concern—" she began.

"He died yesterday," Clara said gently.

The air changed.

Lydia swallowed. "Yes. I heard."

Clara's gaze drifted—not to Lydia's face, but to the objects on her desk. A pen worn thin from use. A stapler with a dented corner. A clean rectangle of space where something ledger-sized had obviously been moved recently.

Nimbus's voice dropped. "She's already afraid."

Clara pulled out her gloves. Lydia noticed immediately.

"What are you doing?" Lydia asked, a little too quickly.

"Being careful," Clara said. "I handle old items. It's habit."

Lydia's gaze tracked the gloves like they were suspicious in their own right. Clara didn't explain further. Explanation invited questions, and questions invited attention she didn't want.

Clara reached for the pen.

The echo hit her with clean precision.

Relief—short-lived.

Calculation—steady, practiced.

Fear—sharp and immediate.

And beneath it, the thought that pressed forward with startling clarity:

I needed that money.

Clara kept her face calm. She met Lydia's eyes.

"You were being paid to smooth things over," Clara said quietly. "Permits. Delays. Quiet approvals."

Lydia shook her head too fast. "That's not—"

"Carl stopped," Clara continued. "Two weeks ago."

Something in Lydia's face broke—just a hairline fracture at first, then a widening crack. "He said it wasn't personal," she whispered. "He said the development was done. He said there was no reason to keep—"

"To keep paying," Clara finished softly.

Lydia's shoulders slumped. "I didn't hurt him," she said, voice shaking. "I just went to talk."

Nimbus's tail lashed. "And?"

Clara didn't push harshly. She didn't need to. The truth was already trying to escape.

"What happened next?" Clara asked.

Lydia swallowed hard. "We argued. Not loud. Just... tense. He stood up like he was done with me. He grabbed his chest." Tears spilled before Lydia seemed to realize they were coming. "I thought it was the heart thing. I thought he'd sit back down. I thought he'd—"

Clara's throat tightened. "And you didn't call for help."

Lydia's breath hitched. "I froze."

"Because you were scared," Clara said.

"Yes," Lydia sobbed. "I thought it would come back to me. The payments. The ledger. Everything. I didn't—" She pressed a hand to her mouth. "I didn't want to be the reason everyone looked at me."

Nimbus's voice was quiet now. "And so, you became the reason anyway."

Clara exhaled slowly. "Sheriff Halden will need to hear this."

Lydia nodded, defeated, like she'd been holding the truth under water and finally couldn't anymore.

"I know," she whispered. "I know."

Clara stepped back from the desk, the pen still in her gloved hand like a small, ordinary witness.

Outside the permit office, the cold air felt cleaner. Not kinder—just clearer.

Nimbus looked up at Clara. "Money stopped. Silence didn't."

Clara tucked her hands into her coat pockets, gloves and all. "It never does."

Behind them, the county building hummed with its fluorescent indifference, papers stacked and stamped and filed like they were the only things that mattered.

In Briar Hollow, someone had decided numbers were safer than truth.

Clara had just proven they weren't.

Chapter Five

What Counts as Quiet

Sheriff Halden didn't look surprised.

That was the first thing Clara noticed when Lydia Marsh finally stopped talking long enough to breathe.

He sat behind his desk with his sleeves rolled up, pen resting loosely between his fingers, posture calm in a way that said he'd heard every version of fear people could offer and still expected the truth to fit inside it. His office smelled faintly of paper and winter air—someone had opened a window earlier, as if fresh cold could rinse the room clean.

Lydia sat across from him, shoulders hunched, eyes swollen and red. Her hands twisted together in her lap like they were trying to wring out what she'd done.

Clara stood off to the side—close enough to be part of it, far enough to be sure she wasn't steering it. She kept her face neutral and her hands still. This wasn't her role now. This was the part where the town's quiet habits met something official and unforgiving.

Nimbus sat on the narrow credenza beneath the window, tail wrapped tight around his paws, watching Halden with interest.

"That's a man who hates paperwork but loves clarity," he murmured.

Halden closed his notebook with a soft, final sound.

"You didn't intend to kill him," Halden said evenly, voice low but firm. "But you created the conditions that led to his death. And you chose not to call for help."

Lydia's lips trembled. "I was afraid."

Halden didn't raise his voice. He didn't have to. "Fear explains things. It doesn't excuse them."

He stood and gestured toward the door. "We'll continue this downtown."

Lydia rose slowly, like her legs didn't trust the floor. She didn't resist. Resistance would've required believing there was still a version of this where she didn't end up in trouble.

She glanced once at Clara. Not anger. Not accusation. Just that bleak, sick realization that a private decision had become a public consequence.

Then she walked out with Halden.

When the door shut, Clara felt the office exhale. The silence afterward was different—cleaner. Not peaceful, but not vibrating anymore.

Halden returned a moment later, alone. He set the folder on his desk and looked at Clara with a kind of exhausted professionalism.

"You brought me something solid," he said.

Clara kept her voice careful. "I brought you a pattern."

Halden's mouth tightened like he didn't like the word *pattern* because it implied this wasn't the first, and wouldn't be the last. "That too."

He studied her for a beat. "You didn't bring the ledger in, did you?"

"No," Clara said. "It's locked up."

Halden nodded once. "Good. I'll need it logged." He paused, then added, "And Clara—don't tell me how you found your pattern. I'm not asking. That's on purpose."

Clara's throat tightened. "Understood."

Nimbus's tail flicked. "He's building a little shelf in his brain labeled *Don't Ask Whitlock*."

Halden reached for another paper in his folder. "Carl Benton's autopsy confirmed stress-induced cardiac failure. Triggered by confrontation."

Clara let out a slow breath she hadn't realized she'd been holding. "So, it wasn't staged."

"No," Halden said. "Just pressured." His eyes held hers. "That doesn't make it harmless."

Nimbus murmured, "Pressure kills more cleanly than knives."

Halden didn't react to the cat's voice, but his gaze sharpened as if he felt the same truth without needing words. "This town has a habit of smoothing things over," he said. "Today, it doesn't get to."

Clara nodded. "Thank you."

Halden gave a rough little laugh. "Don't thank me yet. People don't like losing their shortcuts."

He walked her to the door, then stopped with his hand on the knob. "If anyone comes sniffing around your shop—anyone you don't recognize—call me."

Clara's pulse ticked up. "You mean besides the usual sniffers."

Halden's expression didn't shift much, but there was a grim humor in his eyes. "Besides them."

By the time Clara returned to *Second Chances Antiques*, the afternoon light had shifted. Sun angled through the front window, turning dust motes into floating sparks. The shop looked harmless from the outside—just a cozy little place full of forgotten things. But Clara had learned that forgotten didn't mean safe.

She unlocked the door and stepped in.

Nimbus jumped onto the counter and immediately took his position facing the street, like a sentry. "If we're being watched," he said, "I'd like them to feel judged."

Clara set her keys down. "You do that naturally."

Nimbus's ears twitched. "Thank you."

Clara went to the cabinet and retrieved the ledger. She didn't open it. Not now. She didn't need its echo to confirm what she already knew: money had been flowing, then stopped, and someone had panicked hard enough to let a man die.

She wrapped the ledger in brown paper again, tied it with twine, and set it under the counter for Halden to collect.

Nimbus watched her hands. "You see the pattern yet?"

Clara paused. "Silence costs something."

Nimbus nodded once. "And eventually, someone can't afford it."

The bell over the door chimed.

Clara's head snapped up.

A man stood just inside the entrance—mid-thirties, neat jacket, shoes too clean for the icy slush outside. His smile was polite and practiced, the kind that didn't waste energy. His eyes moved across the shelves without truly seeing the objects, like he was evaluating the room rather than shopping in it.

"Afternoon," he said. "I'm looking for something specific."

Clara returned the smile, every instinct tightening. "What's that?"

"Things that tell stories people don't want told."

Nimbus's fur lifted along his spine. "That's not a customer."

Clara stayed behind the counter. No stepping forward. No inviting tone. "You're looking for a different kind of shop."

The man's smile widened just a fraction. "So, it seems."

He didn't argue. He didn't ask for her name. He didn't pretend to browse. He simply held her gaze for a long beat—measuring, curious—then nodded like he'd confirmed what he came to confirm.

He turned and left.

The bell chimed again, cheerful and wrong.

Clara stood very still.

Nimbus stared at the door. "That," he said, "is going to be a problem later."

Clara swallowed. "He wasn't from town."

Nimbus's tail flicked. "No. And he wasn't surprised either."

Clara looked down at the wrapped ledger under the counter.

The money trail was done.

The confession was recorded.

But someone had noticed the way it ended.

And that kind of attention never came quietly.

Chapter Six

What Doesn't Stay Buried

The man didn't come back.

Clara told herself that should have been a relief.

It wasn't.

Briar Hollow had patterns. Predictable ones. People circled the same questions, the same rumors, the same grudges, until everything either dissolved into boredom or hardened into certainty. Strangers, especially, rarely did anything once. They checked a place. They checked a person. Then they checked again.

This man had walked in, said the kind of sentence that didn't belong in a normal antique shop, and left like he'd only needed to confirm she existed.

Then he vanished.

Nimbus spent most of the afternoon posted in the front window, body still, eyes active, tail occasionally ticking with displeasure. He watched every person who passed like he was evaluating whether they had a motive, an alibi, or a conscience.

"That one's lying to someone," he said as an older woman hurried across the street with a leather bag.

Clara, rearranging a display of china cups that had already been arranged twice, didn't look up. "How can you tell?"

Nimbus's ears twitched. "She's walking like she's late to a conversation."

A teenager cut across the square, hood up, hands jammed deep into pockets.

Nimbus's tail flicked once. "That one's stealing something. Probably not from you, but still."

Clara sighed. "You're exhausting."

Nimbus didn't blink. "I'm accurate."

Clara tried to keep the shop open as normal. She really did. She flipped the sign to *Open*, straightened the brass lamps, polished the glass case, and pretended she was just a woman with a quirky shop and a moody cat.

But the day refused to behave.

Customers came in, browsed without seeing, and left empty-handed. When they spoke, they spoke in that careful, coded way small towns used when tragedy sat too close.

"Such a shame," one woman murmured, lifting a porcelain bird only to set it back down as if it were suddenly fragile.

"Yes," Clara said, because that was the only safe response.

"Oh, and—did you hear?" the woman added, eyes flicking toward the door like gossip could be arrested.

Clara did not ask what she'd heard. She didn't need to.

By early afternoon, the diner down the street sent the smell of fried potatoes drifting through the square. The town's metabolism shifted—lunch, chatter, an attempt to keep going.

Clara watched it all through her front window and felt the strange disconnect of being both inside and outside at once.

Nimbus jumped down from the window and padded behind the counter, brushing against her ankle with the casual possessiveness of a creature who did not ask permission to belong.

"You're spiraling," he said.

"I'm working," Clara replied.

Nimbus's eyes narrowed. "You're pretending that if you keep your hands busy, your head will stop counting."

Clara froze, cloth in hand. "I don't—"

Nimbus hopped onto the counter. "You do. You count risks. You count exits. You count how long it's been since the bell rang. You're practically a ledger yourself."

Clara's throat tightened. She set the cloth down slowly. "I don't like being watched."

Nimbus's ears angled forward. "Then stop acting like you're alone."

The bell over the door chimed.

Clara's entire body tightened before she could stop it.

But it wasn't the stranger. It was Sheriff Halden.

He stepped inside without ceremony, coat collar turned up against the cold, face drawn in the way it got when he'd spent the day cutting through people's excuses.

Nimbus's tail flicked. "Ah. The human with the badge."

Halden didn't glance at Nimbus, but his eyes landed on Clara and held. "You all right?"

Clara forced herself to breathe. "I'm aware."

Halden gave a faint, humorless smile. "That's usually how it starts."

He moved to the counter. "I'm here for the ledger."

Clara nodded and reached under the counter to retrieve the wrapped bundle. Brown paper, twine. Evidence disguised as something ordinary.

Halden took it carefully, and Clara watched his hands—gloved, steady. He was the type of man who respected objects the way he respected guns: not because they were sacred, but because they were dangerous when misunderstood.

"Lydia Marsh is being booked," Halden said. "Voluntary manslaughter. Failure to render aid."

Clara's stomach dipped anyway. The charge wasn't a shock, but the finality of it was.

"And Carl?" she asked.

Halden exhaled through his nose. "Official cause stands. Stress-induced cardiac failure. Triggered by confrontation." He paused. "It doesn't look clean on paper. But it's the truth."

Nimbus's voice was low. "Truth rarely flatters anyone."

Halden glanced toward the window, toward the street. "Town's already trying to decide what this means."

Clara's mouth tightened. "What do they want it to mean?"

Halden's eyes narrowed slightly. "They want it to mean it's over."

Clara didn't respond. She didn't trust herself to say what she was thinking—that in Briar Hollow, *over* was just the word people used when they were tired.

Halden shifted the ledger under one arm. "You hear from anyone... unusual... you call me."

Clara's pulse ticked up. "I had a man come in earlier."

Halden's posture sharpened. "Describe him."

Clara did—clean jacket, too-alert eyes, wrong kind of smile, wrong kind of question.

Halden's jaw tightened. "You didn't get a name."

"No."

"License plate?"

"No."

Nimbus sighed. "We're bad at surveillance."

Halden held her gaze. "If he comes back, you call immediately. You don't engage."

Clara nodded. "Understood."

Halden paused at the door, hand on the knob. He didn't soften his voice, but it lowered slightly. "Clara."

She looked up.

"Briar Hollow doesn't like mirrors," he said. "You're holding one up. That makes people... unpredictable. They don't like seeing themselves as they really are."

Clara swallowed. "I'm not trying to—"

"I know," Halden said, and there was something almost kind in the way he said it. "Still. Be careful."

Then he left.

The bell chimed cheerfully behind him, as if the shop hadn't just absorbed another warning.

Clara locked the door immediately after he was gone, even though it wasn't closing time yet.

Nimbus watched her. "You're closing early."

"I'm thinking," Clara said.

Nimbus hopped down to the floor and sat, looking up at her. "And what do you think?"

Clara stared at the street through the glass. People passed. Cars rolled by. Life continued with its practiced indifference.

"I think," she said slowly, "that the ledger wasn't the only thing someone was keeping track of."

Nimbus's eyes gleamed. "There it is."

Clara turned the sign to *CLOSED* and killed the overhead lights, leaving only the softer lamps glowing around the shop. Shadows gathered in the corners, making the antiques look like they were listening.

She breathed once, twice, trying to convince her body it was safe.

The bell chimed.

Both of them froze.

The door did not open.

Something slid across the threshold and stopped at Clara's feet with a soft scrape.

A small parcel.

No knock.

No voice.

No footsteps retreating.

Just the package, placed like a message.

Nimbus's fur rose along his spine. "No."

Clara didn't touch it right away. She crouched slowly, studying it where it lay, as if it might suddenly move on its own.

Brown paper, neatly wrapped. Twine tied tight. No return address. One word written in careful ink, all caps like a label.

FOR WHITLOCK

Her throat tightened.

Nimbus's voice dropped to a whisper. "That's not coincidence."

Clara slipped on her gloves with shaking hands—not dramatic shaking, but controlled. The kind of shaking that came from adrenaline being told it had to behave.

She lifted the parcel.

It wasn't heavy, but it had weight—the kind that came from intent.

She carried it to the counter and set it down gently, like something sleeping.

She didn't open it.

Not yet.

Nimbus stared at it like it had personally offended him. "Whatever that is," he said, "it's not from town."

Clara swallowed. "No."

Outside, Briar Hollow hummed with evening sounds—cars, laughter from the diner, a radio playing too loud somewhere it shouldn't. The town was already trying to normalize what had happened, smoothing the edges, rewriting the discomfort into something easier to swallow.

Inside, Clara stood very still behind her counter.

Because silence had a cost.

And someone—somewhere—had decided she was worth paying attention to.

She turned the sign to **CLOSED** (again, as if it could seal the door against intention), reached for the light switch, and let the shop fall into deeper shadow.

Tomorrow, she'd open the package.

Tonight, she let it wait.

Chapter Seven

What the Quiet Leaves Behind

The town didn't say thank you.

Clara hadn't expected it to.

Two days after Lydia Marsh was taken into custody, Briar Hollow adjusted its posture the way it always did—shoulders back, chin up, eyes forward. The story settled into place with a new vocabulary: *unfortunate*, *misunderstanding*, *stress*. The sharper words were quietly retired.

Clara watched it happen from behind the counter at *Second Chances Antiques*.

Customers returned slowly, cautiously, like animals testing whether a storm had truly passed. They browsed. They chatted. They avoided looking directly at her for too long.

Nimbus lay stretched across the front window, tail flicking occasionally. "They've decided you're safe again," he said.

"For how long?" Clara asked.

Nimbus cracked one eye open. "Depends on whether you keep reminding them."

Clara adjusted a display of old postcards—scenes of Briar Hollow from decades past. Smiling people. Empty streets. A version of the town that had never existed as neatly as the photographs suggested.

The bell chimed.

Vesta Rowe stepped inside.

She looked smaller than the last time Clara had seen her, grief pressing her inward like weather. She hesitated near the door, hands clenched around her purse strap.

Clara came out from behind the counter. "You don't have to—"

"I wanted to," Vesta said quickly. "Before I talked myself out of it."

They stood there for a moment, surrounded by objects that had survived longer than most regrets.

"I know people are saying things," Vesta said. "About Carl. About what he did. About what Lydia did." Her jaw tightened. "I don't care."

Clara waited.

Vesta met her eyes. "He wasn't perfect. He was... controlling. Careful. Always trying to make problems go away with money." She swallowed. "But he didn't deserve to die like that."

"No," Clara said softly. "He didn't."

Vesta exhaled shakily. "Thank you for not letting them pretend it was nothing."

Clara felt the weight of that land. "It wasn't nothing."

Vesta nodded once, satisfied, and left without another word.

Nimbus watched the door close. "That one mattered."

Clara leaned against the counter, suddenly tired in a way sleep didn't fix.

That afternoon, Sheriff Halden stopped by without warning.

He didn't stay long.

"Paperwork's done," he said. "Charges are official."

Clara nodded. "And the town?"

Halden's mouth twitched. "Already rewriting itself."

Nimbus snorted. "Talented like that."

Halden hesitated. "I wanted you to know... some people are unhappy."

Clara met his gaze. "I assumed."

"But," Halden continued, "some people are relieved." He paused. "They just won't say it out loud."

Clara absorbed that quietly.

Halden moved toward the door, then stopped. "About the man you mentioned."

Clara's pulse ticked up. "Yes?"

"I asked around," Halden said. "No one recognizes him. No plates caught. No record of him in town that day."

Nimbus's fur bristled. "Of course not."

Halden looked at Clara seriously. "That doesn't sit right with me."

"It doesn't sit right with me either," Clara said.

Halden nodded once. "Just... don't go looking for trouble."

Clara didn't promise.

That evening, after the shop was closed and the town lights softened into their nighttime glow, Clara stood alone behind the counter.

The parcel sat where she'd left it.

Unopened.

Nimbus watched her from the stool. "You're still not going to open it, are you?"

"Not tonight," Clara said.

"Good," Nimbus replied. "Anticipation is educational."

Clara smiled faintly. "You're enjoying this."

Nimbus's eyes gleamed. "I enjoy preparedness."

Clara reached out and rested her hand—not on the parcel, but on the counter beside it. She didn't need to touch it to feel its presence. Pride. Intention. Expectation.

Someone had seen what she did.

Not the town.

Not the sheriff.

Someone else.

Clara squared her shoulders.

She hadn't asked to become a mirror.

But she wouldn't look away now that she was one.

Nimbus hopped down and brushed against her leg. "You're going to keep doing this."

Clara nodded. "Yes."

Nimbus's tail flicked. "Good. Because quiet never stays quiet forever."

Clara turned off the last light, leaving the parcel in shadow.

Tomorrow would come with questions.

Tonight, she let the truth sit where it belonged—acknowledged, uncomfortable, and impossible to ignore.

Bloodline Blush in Briar Hollow

The Quiet Discretion Mysteries - Book Three

Petra Shaw

CSD Digital Enterprises, LLC

Chapter One

Bloodline Blush in Briar Hollow

Clara Whitlock left the parcel exactly where she had put it two days ago.

Right on the shelf of *Second Chances Antiques*.

She didn't open it that night.

She didn't open it the next morning either.

Not because she was afraid—Clara told herself she wasn't afraid anymore—but because she'd learned that some things became louder when you touched them. And this package had already managed to fill the shop with a kind of attention she didn't want to invite.

Nimbus watched it from the counter like it was a sleeping animal.

"It's still there," he observed.

Clara hung up her coat with slow precision. "Yes."

"You're stalling."

"I'm thinking."

Nimbus's tail flicked. "Thinking is just stalling with better posture."

Clara didn't argue. She set her keys down and turned the sign to *Closed* even though the sun wasn't fully up yet. The town could wait. If anyone complained, she'd blame inventory.

Inventory was a safe word. People respected safe words.

She approached the parcel and crouched. Brown paper. Twine. No return address. The inked label still looked too crisp.

FOR WHITLOCK

Clara slipped on her gloves.

Nimbus hopped down and circled once, sniffing the air. "Whatever this is," he muttered, "it's proud of itself."

Clara froze. "Proud?"

Nimbus's eyes narrowed. "It's not hiding. It's posing."

That sent a cold ripple through her chest.

Clara lifted the parcel and carried it to the counter as if it might suddenly decide to move on its own. She set it down gently, then untied the twine. The knot loosened without resistance, as if whoever tied it had wanted it opened quickly—wanted her hands on it.

The paper peeled back in neat folds.

Inside was a small velvet pouch the color of dried roses, and beneath it, a note on stiff cream paper.

Clara didn't touch the pouch yet.

She read the note first.

Three words, written in careful script:

Look closer, Whitlock.

Nimbus made a sound between a snort and a growl. "I hate being invited."

Clara folded the note and set it aside. Then she lifted the velvet pouch and turned it over once in her hands.

The echo brushed her even through the fabric.

Not panic.

Not grief.

Something firmer.

A straight-backed feeling. Chin lifted. A hand on a shoulder.

Protection.

And behind it—like a shadow following too closely—fear.

Clara's throat tightened.

"Family," Nimbus said softly.

Clara glanced at him. "You're guessing."

"I'm not," Nimbus replied. "I'm smelling it."

She opened the pouch.

A cameo brooch slid into her gloved palm.

Oval. Classic. The enamel portrait was a woman's profile—soft curls, pale throat, a calm expression that felt almost smug. The gold frame was tarnished in the grooves, and the pin on the back had been repaired once, crudely, as if someone had refused to stop wearing it even when it broke.

A thin crack ran through the enamel like a lightning strike.

Clara stared at the face in the portrait.

It wasn't anyone she recognized.

But the echo hit hard the moment she fully registered the brooch.

Pride—dense and deliberate.

Protection—tight as a hand clamped over a mouth.

Then a flare of panic so sharp it made Clara's breath catch.

Her vision didn't blur. She didn't lose her footing.

But the shop felt smaller.

Like the walls had shifted closer to listen.

Clara set the brooch down on the velvet pouch, still gloved, and forced herself to breathe through the aftertaste of someone else's fear.

Nimbus leaned in, eyes narrowing. "That crack isn't age."

Clara swallowed. "No."

It felt like a moment.

A single moment where everything had tipped.

A secret threatened. A decision made fast.

Clara glanced back at the portrait. The woman looked serene, like she'd never broken a rule in her life.

"Do you know her?" Nimbus asked.

Clara shook her head. "Not from the face."

Nimbus's tail flicked. "Then she's not the point."

Clara's pulse ticked steadily now, controlled.

She reached for a magnifying glass from beneath the counter and held it over the brooch, scanning the edge of the frame. Tiny initials had been engraved on the back near the pin's repaired hinge.

Not a name.

Just two letters.

E. R.

Clara sat very still.

Nimbus watched her expression. "What?"

Clara didn't answer right away. She was listening to the echo again, now that the first wave had passed.

Protection.

Not for a town.

Not for money.

For someone specific.

Someone who belonged.

Or someone who wasn't supposed to.

Clara lifted her gaze to the shop window. Outside, Briar Hollow was waking up. Cars moved slow over cold pavement. A woman crossed the square with a pastry box balanced on one palm. The diner's lights flickered on like nothing had ever happened.

The town looked ordinary.

Which meant, almost certainly, it wasn't.

Clara picked up the note again.

Look closer, Whitlock.

Nimbus's voice lowered. "Who sent it?"

Clara set the note down, careful. "Someone who wants me to pull a thread."

Nimbus's ears flattened slightly. "Or someone who wants you wrapped in it."

Clara's stomach tightened.

She slid the brooch back into the pouch and tucked the pouch into the cabinet under the counter, locking it away like evidence she hadn't earned yet.

Nimbus watched her. "You're not going to follow it?"

"I am," Clara said.

"Today?"

Clara looked at the shop clock. Then at the door.

"Today," she confirmed. "Before the town decides what story it wants."

Nimbus's eyes gleamed. "And what story is that?"

Clara's voice went quiet. "The one where family is sacred and questions are rude."

Nimbus hopped onto the counter and settled beside her like a shadow that chose loyalty.

"Then let's be rude," he said.

Clara turned the sign to *Open*.

And outside, Briar Hollow kept smiling—unaware that a cracked little brooch had just arrived to prove that blood could be quiet too.

Chapter Two

What the Brooch Remembers

C lara didn't trust the cameo brooch to stay quiet just because she'd locked it away.

Objects didn't get quieter when you ignored them.

They got patient.

She spent the first hour after opening the shop pretending to do ordinary things—dusting the shelves, straightening a rack of vintage postcards, reorganizing the glass case by size and fragility. It was busy-work with a purpose: it gave her hands a rhythm while her mind sorted what she'd felt.

Protection.

Not the warm kind.

The tight kind. The kind that said *mine* and meant it.

Nimbus watched her from the counter, chin on his paws, eyes half-lidded like he was bored.

"You're circling," he said.

"I'm thinking," Clara replied.

Nimbus's tail flicked. "Again, yes."

Clara ignored him and waited until the shop had its first real customer—a man hunting for a lamp shade—then its second—a woman browsing framed photographs without seeing any of them. When the door finally closed behind the second customer and the bell's cheerful chime faded, Clara flipped the sign to *Closed* without apology.

Nimbus lifted his head. "Already?"

"I need quiet," Clara said.

Nimbus looked around the shop. "You run an antique store. Quiet is literally your brand."

"You know what I mean."

Nimbus hopped down and followed her to the counter cabinet like he was escorting her to a crime scene.

Clara unlocked the cabinet, took out the velvet pouch, and set it on the counter. She slipped on her gloves again, slower this time. More deliberate. Then she opened the pouch and lifted the cameo brooch into her palm.

The echo didn't explode the way it had the first time.

It settled.

Like a weight on her chest.

Pride came first—a posture, a practiced smile. The kind that could stand in a church aisle or a funeral line and look unshakable.

Then protection. Stronger now that she was listening for it.

A hand pressed to a child's back. A whispered instruction. A door closing.

And beneath it, pulsing like a heartbeat someone was trying to hide—

Fear.

Clara's breath caught, not from shock this time but from clarity. The fear wasn't about being hurt.

It was about being exposed.

Nimbus leaned closer. "Tell me it's not what I think."

"You haven't told me what you think."

Nimbus's eyes narrowed. "It's family."

Clara swallowed. "Yes."

Nimbus's tail lashed once. "Of course it is."

Clara lowered the brooch onto the velvet pouch and took the magnifying glass again. She studied the crack in the enamel. It wasn't just time-worn. It had direction—an impact point, then a split that ran like lightning through the portrait's cheek and down toward the neck.

"This broke during a moment," Clara murmured.

Nimbus sniffed. "A moment someone remembers too clearly."

Clara turned the brooch over. The repaired pin back was uneven, soldered by someone who cared more about keeping it wearable than keeping it pretty. And the initials—**E. R.**—sat near the hinge like a quiet signature.

"Do those letters mean anything?" Nimbus asked.

"Not yet."

Nimbus's ears twitched. "Yet is ominous."

Clara touched the initials lightly with her gloved fingertip.

The echo sharpened.

A woman's voice—firm, low—cut through memory like a blade.

We don't tell anyone.

Not even them.

This is family business.

Clara flinched, not physically, but internally—like a door had been slammed in her face from decades away.

Then another sensation: a small body being guided forward. A child, maybe a baby. The careful shifting of blankets. A pressed kiss on a forehead.

Protection.

A promise.

And then—fear again, sudden and sharp, like the realization that promises could fail.

Nimbus went very still. "That's a child."

Clara's throat tightened. "Yes."

Nimbus's voice dropped. "Not supposed to exist."

Clara didn't answer, because the brooch answered for her.

The echo showed her a room: lace curtains, a dresser, a mirror reflecting lamplight. Someone's hands trembled over paperwork. A pen scratched. A name changed.

Not erased.

Replaced.

Clara pulled her hand back.

The shop felt too quiet now. Even the old wooden floors seemed to hold their breath.

Nimbus watched her face. "Adoption."

Clara nodded slowly. "Or something they made look like blood."

Nimbus's tail flicked. "And people kill to keep that kind of lie intact."

Clara set the brooch down and stared at the portrait again. The woman's face looked calm, even kind.

It was always the calm ones.

Clara forced herself to breathe evenly and pulled the note from yesterday off the counter.

Look closer, Whitlock.

It didn't feel like a threat.

It felt like a nudge.

A push.

Like someone wanted the truth found—not out of justice, but out of spite.

Nimbus's ears angled forward. "Whoever sent that parcel... they're not doing it to help."

Clara folded the note. "No. They're doing it to aim me."

Nimbus hopped up onto the counter again, closer than before. "So don't be aimed."

Clara looked at him. "How?"

Nimbus's eyes gleamed. "You aim yourself."

Clara exhaled slowly.

She looked at the initials again. **E. R.**

Then she looked at the town outside her front window—people moving like everything was normal, like peace was something you could declare and it would become true.

"E.R.," Clara murmured. "If those are a person's initials, the easiest way to find them is through someone who talks too much."

Nimbus's mouth curled. "June."

Clara nodded.

Nimbus jumped down. "Then let's go before the diner fills with people practicing silence."

Clara slipped the brooch back into its pouch, locked it away, and grabbed her coat.

As she turned toward the door, the bell above it gave a small, harmless chime—just the shop settling, just the building breathing.

But Clara didn't miss how the sound seemed to echo slightly longer than usual.

As if the shop itself was listening.

As if the brooch had woken something that liked being kept quiet.

And Briar Hollow—smiling, ordinary Briar Hollow—was about to find out that family secrets didn't stay buried.

Not once someone decided to look closer.

Chapter Three

Another Peaceful Passing

T he news broke before Clara reached the diner.

     She knew it by the way Briar Hollow had already adjusted its voice.

People didn't stop talking when something happened. They changed *how* they talked—lower, smoother, like they were sanding down a rough edge before it could catch. The town square carried that sound now, a soft murmur that slid past details and lingered on conclusions.

Nimbus padded beside her, tail low. "Hear that?"

"Yes," Clara said. "They've agreed on a word."

They stepped inside the diner, and the bell chimed too brightly for the mood. June looked up from behind the counter, saw Clara, and her face tightened just enough to be honest.

"Sit," June said, already reaching for the cinnamon sticks. "Before you hear it wrong."

Clara slid onto her usual stool. Nimbus took the empty one beside her, unseen and uninvited as always.

June leaned in. "Eleanor Ridgeway died this morning."

Clara's stomach dipped. "Eleanor?"

June nodded. "In her sleep. That's what they're saying."

Nimbus exhaled softly. "There it is."

Clara kept her voice steady. "Who found her?"

"Her granddaughter," June said. "Came by to check on her before work. Called it in. Sheriff's there now."

Eleanor Ridgeway. The name settled with weight.

Old family. Old money. Old influence, even if the money wasn't what it used to be. Eleanor had chaired committees, hosted fundraisers, and corrected people gently when they got town history wrong. She was the kind of woman people described as *pillarlike*—something solid you leaned on without ever asking if it wanted the weight.

"Peaceful?" Clara asked quietly.

June nodded once. "Very."

Nimbus's tail flicked. "Of course it was."

Clara glanced around the diner. Conversations continued, but no one laughed too loudly. No one said Eleanor's name more than once per sentence. Grief was being handled carefully, like a dish that chipped easily.

June wiped the counter again, though it was already clean. "They're saying how lucky she was. To go like that. No suffering."

"Did she have health issues?" Clara asked.

June hesitated. "Nothing sudden."

Nimbus leaned closer to Clara's ear. "That means no."

Clara finished her water and stood. "Thanks, June."

June caught her wrist—not hard, just enough to stop her. "Be careful," she said quietly. "The Ridgeways don't like surprises."

Clara met her eyes. "Neither do I."

Outside, the cold air sharpened her focus.

Nimbus looked up at her. "You thinking what I'm thinking?"

"That the initials might not be about the brooch's owner," Clara said. "They might be about who it was protecting."

Nimbus's ears flattened. "Eleanor Ridgeway."

Clara nodded.

They didn't go straight to Eleanor's house.

That would have been too obvious.

Instead, Clara took the long way around the square, past the library, past the florist already assembling sympathy arrangements, past the bulletin board where a neatly typed notice had appeared as if by magic:

Community Remembrance Gathering — Tonight, 7 p.m.

No questions.

No details.

Just closure scheduled in advance.

Nimbus read it and snorted. "That's efficient."

Clara's jaw tightened. "That's control."

They circled back toward the Ridgeway house from the alley that ran behind it. The property sat at the edge of town like it always had—large enough to notice, modest enough to avoid resentment. The front yard was already full of cars, sheriff's cruiser included.

Clara stopped at the edge of the hedge and didn't move closer.

She didn't need to.

The echo reached her anyway.

Not from the house itself.

From the people.

Grief—real, aching.

Pride—unyielding.

And beneath it, pulsing like a second heartbeat—

Fear.

Clara closed her eyes briefly.

"Same shape," Nimbus murmured. "Different object."

Clara exhaled. "Someone's trying to protect something again."

Nimbus glanced at the house. "Or someone."

A woman stepped out onto the front porch then—mid-thirties, dark hair pulled back too tightly, phone clutched in her hand. She spoke quickly to Halden, her gestures sharp, controlled.

"That's Margaret Ridgeway," Nimbus said. "Eleanor's daughter."

Clara watched carefully.

Margaret didn't cry.

She didn't waver.

She stood between the house and the world like a gate.

"That's not grief," Clara said.

Nimbus's tail flicked. "That's containment."

Clara turned away before anyone noticed her watching.

The town already had its story.

Eleanor Ridgeway had died peacefully.

Anything else would be rude.

Clara walked back toward her shop, the weight of the brooch heavy even though it was locked away.

Two "peaceful" deaths. Carl Benton last week. And now, Eleanor Ridgeway.

Two secrets.

And one town that kept choosing quiet over truth.

Nimbus broke the silence. "You're in it now."

Clara didn't disagree.

Because Eleanor Ridgeway hadn't just died.

She'd taken something with her.

And Briar Hollow was going to make sure no one asked what it was.

Chapter Four

The Family Wall

C lara waited until afternoon to approach the Ridgeway house.

Grief had schedules in Briar Hollow. Mornings were for discovery and shock. Midday was for coordination. Afternoon was when people stopped answering questions they didn't like and started pretending they were busy.

She chose afternoon on purpose.

Nimbus padded beside her up the curved walk, tail low, posture alert. "They'll be ready."

"For me?" Clara asked.

Nimbus's ears twitched. "For anyone."

The Ridgeway house was quiet in the way expensive houses often were—not empty, just controlled. Curtains drawn halfway. Cars parked with care. A wreath already hung on the door, pale flowers arranged into something tasteful and distant.

Clara rang the bell.

It chimed once. Clear. Unapologetic.

Footsteps followed almost immediately.

Margaret Ridgeway opened the door.

Up close, she looked even more contained than she had from a distance—hair pinned precisely, makeup minimal, eyes sharp and dry. She took in Clara in one quick scan, cataloging her coat, her gloves, the fact that she'd come alone.

"Yes?" Margaret said.

Clara offered a polite smile. "I'm Clara Whitlock. I own the antique shop on the square."

Margaret's eyes flicked once toward Nimbus's position beside Clara, then back to Clara's face. "I know who you are."

That wasn't a greeting.

"I wanted to offer my condolences," Clara said. "Eleanor meant a lot to this town."

Margaret nodded once. "She did."

She made no move to invite Clara in.

Clara didn't push. "I also wondered if Eleanor ever brought anything to my shop. A brooch, perhaps."

Margaret's expression didn't change.

But the echo flared.

Pride—tight and polished.

Fear—immediate and sharp.

And beneath it, something colder.

Calculation.

Margaret's voice stayed level. "My mother didn't collect trinkets."

Nimbus's tail flicked. "Lie."

Clara kept her tone neutral. "This wouldn't have been a purchase. More of a... keepsake."

Margaret's jaw tightened almost imperceptibly. "You should leave."

The words weren't loud. They didn't need to be.

Clara nodded. "Of course."

She took one step back, then paused. "I'm sorry for your loss."

Margaret held her gaze for a beat too long. "We value privacy," she said. "I'm sure you understand."

Clara did understand.

She turned and walked away without another word.

Nimbus waited until they were halfway down the path. "That's a wall."

"Yes," Clara said quietly. "And it's been standing a long time."

They didn't make it to the sidewalk before a voice called out behind them.

"Clara."

Clara stopped.

A young woman stood at the side of the house, partially hidden by a bare-limbed dogwood. Early twenties, maybe. Dark hair loose, hands shoved into the pockets of a thick sweater like she wasn't sure what to do with them.

Margaret Ridgeway's daughter.

"Hi," the young woman said quickly, glancing toward the front door. "I'm Barbara."

Clara turned fully. "Hello, Barbara."

Barbara hesitated, then blurted, "You asked about a brooch."

Clara didn't answer immediately.

She didn't want to scare her.

Nimbus leaned closer. "Careful."

"Yes," Clara said gently. "I did."

Barbara swallowed. "My grandmother wore it sometimes. Not often. Just... when it mattered."

Clara felt the echo stir even without the object present. "Do you know where it is now?"

Barbara shook her head. "No. It's gone." Her voice dropped. "I noticed this morning."

Clara's pulse quickened. "Before or after...?"

"Before," Barbara said. "I think."

Nimbus's ears flattened. "Someone moved fast."

Barbara hugged herself. "My mother says I'm imagining things."

Clara met her eyes. "Are you?"

Barbara shook her head harder. "No. She told me once—my grandmother—that the brooch meant *family*. That it reminded her who belonged."

Clara's throat tightened. "Who belonged where?"

Barbara's eyes flicked toward the house again. "Exactly."

Footsteps sounded on the porch.

Margaret's voice cut through the air, crisp and controlled. "Barbara."

Barbara flinched.

"I should go," she whispered. "Please... don't make this worse."

Clara nodded. "I won't."

Barbara hurried back toward the house, shoulders hunched.

Margaret watched her go, then turned her gaze on Clara—cold now, stripped of politeness.

"I asked you to leave," Margaret said.

"And I am," Clara replied calmly. "I just needed to know whether the brooch existed."

Margaret stepped closer. "You don't need to know anything about my family."

Nimbus's voice was low. "That's never true."

Clara met Margaret's stare. "Then you don't need to worry about me."

Margaret held the silence, testing it.

Finally, she said, "Goodbye, Ms. Whitlock."

The door closed firmly.

Clara stood on the sidewalk for a moment longer, letting the echo settle.

"That wasn't grief," Nimbus said again.

"No," Clara replied. "That was defense."

Nimbus glanced back at the house. "And defenses mean something's under attack."

Clara turned toward town, the image of the cracked cameo clear in her mind.

Someone had taken the brooch.

Someone had decided it mattered more than mourning.

And the Ridgeway family wasn't just protecting the past.

They were protecting who got to inherit it.

Clara headed back toward her shop, already planning her next move.

Because walls were meant to keep people out.

And she now knew exactly where to push.

Chapter Five

Halden's Line

Sheriff Halden didn't invite Clara to sit.

He stood behind his desk with his jacket still on, one hand braced against the edge like he was anchoring himself to something solid. The office smelled faintly of cold air and paper—someone had opened the window again, letting winter scrub at the room without much success.

Nimbus hopped onto the narrow shelf beneath the window and curled his tail neatly around his paws.

"This is a standing conversation," he murmured. "Those are never good."

Halden looked up as Clara stepped inside. His expression was careful—not closed, but guarded, like a man deciding how much truth he could afford to exchange.

"You went to the Ridgeway house," he said.

Clara didn't pretend surprise. "Yes."

Halden exhaled slowly. "That family doesn't appreciate visits."

"They don't appreciate questions," Clara corrected.

Halden's mouth tightened. "Same difference, to them."

He gestured toward the chair opposite his desk, then stopped himself. He stayed standing. Clara remained where she was.

"This is where I tell you to stop," Halden said.

Clara met his eyes. "You're not going to arrest me."

"No," Halden said. "I'm going to warn you."

Nimbus's tail flicked. "He means it."

Halden folded his arms. "Eleanor Ridgeway's death is still under review. No signs of forced entry. No toxins. No trauma." He paused. "And a family that hired counsel before the coroner finished."

"That's not grief," Clara said softly.

"That's influence," Halden replied. "And influence makes things... delicate."

Clara took a measured breath. "The brooch is missing."

Halden's gaze sharpened. "What brooch?"

Clara hesitated—just a fraction.

Nimbus leaned forward. "Careful."

"A cameo," Clara said. "Oval. Enamel. Cracked."

Halden didn't react immediately. Then: "That wasn't in the initial inventory."

"Because it wasn't there," Clara said. "It was taken."

Halden rubbed a hand over his jaw. "You're certain."

"Yes."

He studied her for a long moment, weighing something that wasn't written down. "And you're tying this to Carl Benton now. Because—

"Carl Benton? No, I'm tying it to silence," Clara said. "Different reasons. Same outcome."

Halden looked toward the window, the square visible beyond it. "Briar Hollow protects its own."

"So did Carl," Clara said. "Until he stopped paying."

Halden's jaw clenched. "This isn't about money."

"No," Clara agreed. "It's about inheritance."

That landed.

Halden turned back to her. "You have proof?"

"Not yet."

"Then this stays quiet," Halden said firmly. "Until it decides to make some noise on its own."

Nimbus sighed. "That's the town motto."

Halden shot a brief glance toward Nimbus's position—more instinct than awareness—then back to Clara. "If you push too hard, they'll shut every door."

Clara nodded. "They already have."

Halden's shoulders dropped slightly, like he'd been expecting that answer. "Then listen carefully. If this turns criminal, I can act. If it stays... familial..." He let the sentence trail off.

Clara finished it. "You can't."

Halden nodded once. "That's my line."

Nimbus's voice was quiet. "And she's already crossed it."

Halden stepped closer, lowering his voice. "I'm asking you not to force my hand."

Clara met his gaze steadily. "I'm asking you not to look away."

Silence settled between them, heavy but honest.

Finally, Halden said, "If you find something concrete—something I can put on paper—you come to me first."

Clara inclined her head. "I will."

Halden opened the door. "Be careful, Clara."

She stepped out into the cold air, Nimbus padding beside her.

"Well," Nimbus said, "that was the official version of *please don't make this harder*."

Clara pulled her coat tighter. "I don't intend to."

Nimbus glanced back at the station. "You already are. Let me explain. Two weeks ago, Travis Rowe was killed. Last week Carl Benton died. And this week, Eleanor Ridgeway. In a big city, a death a week would be nothing. But in a small town like Briar Hollow,...it is like dominos falling. One death leads to another, and I think the Sheriff is seeing the same pattern that I do."

Clara looked toward the square, where people moved with careful normalcy, already practicing their smiles for tonight's remembrance gathering. She didn't know what pattern Nimbus and the Sheriff were seeing, she only knew that someone shoved that brooch into her shop which got her involved.

Someone in that family had panicked.

Someone had taken the brooch.

And someone had decided that blood was worth more than truth.

Clara headed back toward her shop, already feeling the pressure building—not loud, not violent.

Just tight.

Like a line being drawn.

And she was standing on the wrong side of it.

Chapter Six

Paper Doesn't Forget

C lara went to the one place Briar Hollow pretended didn't exist when it was inconvenient.

Records.

The town liked its history neat—framed photos, anniversary plaques, stories polished smooth by repetition. But paper remembered differently. Paper kept dates and crossings-out and the quiet moments where something changed shape without anyone announcing it.

Nimbus followed her into the municipal records office with the air of a cat entering enemy territory.

"I hate places where lies are alphabetized," he muttered.

Clara signed the visitor log and took the clipboard the clerk slid across the counter without looking up. The woman didn't ask what she was researching. She didn't want to know. That was the town's second line of defense—don't ask, don't hear.

The records room smelled like dust and lemon cleaner. Rows of metal cabinets lined the walls, each drawer labeled in tidy black letters.

Clara started where she always did.

Births.

Deaths.

Marriages.

She pulled Eleanor Ridgeway's file first.

Everything was exactly where it should be.

Too exactly.

Dates aligned. Signatures clean. No addendums. No corrections. It read like a life that had never required explanation.

Nimbus hopped onto a table and leaned over the folder. "That's suspicious."

"Because it's perfect?" Clara asked quietly.

Nimbus's tail flicked. "Because nothing is."

Clara flipped through older documents—property transfers, trust amendments, charitable donations. The Ridgeways liked paperwork when it benefited them. Eleanor's name appeared everywhere, steady as a watermark.

Then Clara checked the family tree kept on file for historical purposes—submitted decades ago for a centennial celebration.

Eleanor.

Margaret.

Barbara.

No branches. No deviations.

Clara frowned and pulled the drawer again, checking surrounding years.

She found it on the third pass.

A birth record with a familiar date.

Not Eleanor's.

Not Margaret's.

A different name.

Filed under *R*, but crossed out once and rewritten.

The ink didn't match.

Nimbus leaned closer. "There."

Clara's pulse picked up. She examined the form carefully. The original entry listed a baby born in Briar Hollow to a woman whose name had been scratched through with enough pressure to tear the paper slightly.

The replacement name had been written neatly beside it.

Adoption finalized six months later.

Closed record.

Clara sat back slowly.

"That's not normal," Nimbus said.

"No," Clara agreed. "That's curated."

She checked the initials at the bottom of the amended form.

E. R.

Clara closed her eyes briefly.

Protection.

Not of reputation.

Of blood.

She photocopied the page, slid it into her folder, and returned the original exactly where it had been. She didn't need to take more. She already knew how this story worked.

Someone had been born into Briar Hollow.

Someone had been reassigned.

Someone else had decided that family meant paperwork, not truth.

Nimbus jumped down and followed her to the exit. "That's your concrete."

"Yes," Clara said. "Enough to make people nervous."

Nimbus glanced back at the cabinets. "Enough to make them angry."

Outside, the cold hit her face like a warning.

Tonight was the remembrance gathering.

The town would be full.

The family would be watching.

And someone would be carrying a secret that no longer fit where it had been hidden.

Clara headed back toward the square, the copy in her bag heavier than it should have been.

Paper didn't forget.

And neither did she.

The door to the antique shop stood open. Clara rushed in and found only one thing missing—the brooch. She called the Sheriff right away.

Chapter Seven

Blood Isn't Simple

The remembrance gathering filled the square with a careful kind of warmth.

Lanterns hung from hooks that normally held flower baskets. Folding chairs appeared in neat rows, borrowed from the church basement and aligned with the precision of people who wanted things to look respectful. Someone had set up a small podium draped in dark cloth. Someone else had brought cookies no one would eat.

Briar Hollow excelled at public grief.

Clara arrived early and stood at the edge of it all, coat buttoned, hands tucked into her pockets. She didn't bring the photocopy with her. She didn't need it tonight. Tonight wasn't about proof.

It was about pressure.

Nimbus perched invisibly on the low stone wall near the fountain, eyes bright, posture alert.

"This is where they pretend unity," he said. "Watch who stands together."

Clara watched.

The Ridgeways arrived as a unit.

Margaret first—composed, efficient, already greeting people with gentle nods. Barbara followed half a step behind, eyes down, hands clasped tight. Other relatives clustered close, forming a shape that had no gaps.

Containment.

Clara's pulse ticked steady. She didn't approach. Not yet.

She listened.

Speeches began. Soft words about Eleanor's dedication to the town. About her kindness. About her legacy. No mention of complexity. No acknowledgment of flaws. Legacy, Clara noted, was just another word for control once the person was gone.

Nimbus flicked his tail. "They're polishing the statue while it's still warm."

When the applause died down and people began to mingle, Clara moved.

Not toward Margaret.

Toward Barbara.

Barbara stood near the edge of the crowd, half-hidden behind a man Clara recognized as a cousin who talked too loudly when nervous. Barbara's gaze kept drifting—not to the podium, not to the speakers—but to the exit points.

Clara approached slowly, giving her time to see her coming.

Barbara stiffened, then relaxed just enough to prove she'd been expecting this.

"I shouldn't talk to you," Barbara said quietly.

"No," Clara agreed. "You shouldn't."

Barbara's mouth twitched despite herself. "Everyone's watching."

"Everyone's watching Margaret," Clara said. "Not you."

Barbara's shoulders sagged a fraction. "My grandmother wouldn't have wanted this."

Clara tilted her head. "This?"

Barbara gestured vaguely at the lanterns, the speeches, the way people were behaving — like the story had already been finalized. "This version."

Nimbus leaned in. "Good. She's thinking."

Clara lowered her voice. "Did your grandmother ever talk about a child she protected?"

Barbara's breath caught.

Not a gasp.

A hitch.

That was enough.

"I don't know what you're talking about," Barbara said quickly.

Clara didn't push. She simply nodded. "You don't have to tell me."

Barbara swallowed. "My family thinks blood explains everything."

"And you?" Clara asked gently.

Barbara's eyes lifted to the lanterns. "I think blood complicates things."

Clara felt the echo brush her even without an object present—fear mixed with loyalty, stretched thin.

"Your grandmother made a decision," Clara said. "A long time ago."

Barbara's voice dropped to a whisper. "She saved someone."

Clara met her eyes. "And someone else paid for it."

Barbara closed her eyes. "If the truth comes out…"

"Things change," Clara finished. "Inheritance. Names. Belonging."

Barbara nodded once. "My mother would never survive that."

Nimbus murmured, "There it is."

Clara straightened slightly. "Your mother benefits most from silence."

Barbara flinched.

"I don't think she meant for anyone to die," Barbara said, too quickly.

"I don't think so either," Clara replied. "But fear doesn't need intent."

They stood in silence while a new speaker took the podium and began recounting a sanitized story of Eleanor's early years.

Barbara spoke without looking at Clara. "The brooch was gone before morning a couple of days ago."

"Who had access?" Clara asked.

"Family," Barbara said. "Only family, but suddenly it's back."

Clara glanced quickly at the crowd. "Who would have taken it originally?"

Barbara shrugged. "Nobody I know. We all knew it was not to be touched. My mother freaked when you made it known you had it."

That narrowed things cleanly. Neither of them brought the brooch to me. And it was most likely Margaret who took it back.

Margaret's voice carried across the square now, thanking everyone for coming, for respecting privacy, for honoring Eleanor's memory. The word *privacy* landed with the weight of a command.

Barbara's hands curled into fists. "I don't want to be part of this lie."

Clara's voice was steady. "Then don't be."

Barbara looked at her, eyes shining but resolute. "If I tell you where the brooch is..."

Clara didn't interrupt.

Barbara exhaled. "Will you protect the right person?"

Clara held her gaze. "I protect the truth. What people do with it is their choice."

Nimbus's tail flicked approvingly. "That's honest."

Barbara nodded, decision made. "It's in the study. Hidden behind the family portrait."

Clara absorbed that. "Thank you."

Barbara stepped back into the family cluster just as Margaret's eyes flicked toward them, sharp and suspicious.

The line had shifted.

Margaret felt it.

Nimbus's voice dropped. "You've been noticed."

Clara didn't look away. "Good."

Because now she knew where the brooch was.

And more importantly—who had panicked when it disappeared.

Blood wasn't simple.

But lies never were.

And tonight, Briar Hollow's careful quiet had developed a crack—thin, but real.

Just like the enamel in a brooch that was never meant to be seen too closely.

Chapter Eight

The Wrong Target

By morning, Briar Hollow had decided who to blame.

Clara knew it before she heard the name—before the murmurs sharpened into certainty, before the town's collective posture leaned toward relief. Blame, when it arrived quickly, was rarely accurate. It was chosen, not discovered.

Nimbus padded beside her as she crossed the square, tail twitching with irritation.

"They've picked someone," he said. "You can tell by the smiles."

People smiled at her today. Too many of them. The kind of smile that asked for agreement without using words.

"Such a shame," Mrs. Calder said as Clara passed the bakery. "But at least they've figured it out."

"Figured what out?" Clara asked, already knowing.

Mrs. Calder leaned in conspiratorially. "That young man Eleanor was seeing. The one who never quite fit." She shook her head. "Outsiders bring trouble."

Nimbus bared his teeth. "Classic."

Clara kept her voice even. "Who told you that?"

"Oh, you know," Mrs. Calder said breezily. "People talk."

People always did—just not to the right people.

At the diner, the story had hardened.

June slid Clara her mug and sighed. "They're saying Thomas Hale snapped. That he argued with Eleanor the night before she died."

"Did he?" Clara asked.

June hesitated. "He argued with *Margaret*."

That landed.

Nimbus's ears pricked. "Redirect."

June lowered her voice. "Thomas was convenient. No roots here. No history anyone wants to protect."

Clara nodded. "Has anyone actually seen evidence?"

June gave a humorless laugh. "Does that ever stop them?"

Outside, a patrol car idled near the Ridgeway house. Not parked aggressively—just present. A suggestion, not an accusation.

Clara didn't go there yet.

She went to Thomas Hale's rented place instead—a small cottage on the edge of town that still smelled like fresh paint and unclaimed belonging. The door was unlocked. Inside, boxes sat half-unpacked, labeled in careful handwriting.

Nimbus looked around. "He planned to stay."

Clara touched the back of a chair. The echo was faint but clear—confusion, fear, anger that didn't quite know where to land.

No calculation. No relief.

"He didn't do it," Clara said quietly.

Nimbus flicked his tail. "Which is why he's perfect."

A knock sounded at the door.

Clara turned as Halden stepped in, hat in hand. His expression was tight.

"I figured you'd come here," he said.

"Because the story doesn't fit," Clara replied.

Halden nodded once. "He's in questioning. Not under arrest."

"Yet," Nimbus muttered.

Halden glanced around the cottage. "You find anything?"

"Not what you're looking for," Clara said. "But enough to know he's not your culprit."

Halden exhaled slowly. "The family's leaning hard."

"On you," Clara said.

"And on the town," Halden agreed. "They want closure."

Nimbus snorted. "They want containment."

Clara met Halden's gaze. "The brooch is in the Ridgeway house. In the study. Behind the portrait."

Halden stilled.

"That's a very specific place," he said carefully.

"I didn't guess," Clara replied.

Halden studied her for a long beat, then nodded. "All right."

Nimbus's eyes gleamed. "He's choosing."

Halden straightened. "If it's there, and if it ties to inheritance tampering..." He let the sentence finish itself. "I'll need cause."

"You'll have it," Clara said. "Paper remembers."

Halden's jaw tightened. "Then I'll do this clean."

Clara stepped back into the cold air, watching him head toward his cruiser.

Nimbus looked up at her. "You just redirected the story."

"No," Clara said. "I just stopped it from landing where it shouldn't."

Across the square, the Ridgeway house stood quiet and composed, like it always had.

But now the wrong target had been chosen.

And the right one was about to feel the pressure shift.

Because in Briar Hollow, blame was a relief valve.

And someone had just turned it the wrong way.

Chapter Nine

The One Who Panicked

C lara didn't go home.

She went back to her shop and locked the door behind her, leaning into it for a moment longer than necessary. The bell gave a small, harmless chime, and then the quiet settled—thick, expectant.

Nimbus hopped onto the counter and turned a slow circle. "This is the part where everyone realizes their plan has teeth."

Clara nodded. "And someone checks whether theirs is sharper."

She didn't need the brooch in her hands to feel it now. The echo lingered in her bones, steady and insistent—protection straining toward desperation.

She took off her coat, folded it carefully, and waited.

It didn't take long.

The phone rang.

Clara let it ring twice before answering. "Second Chances."

There was a breath on the other end—controlled, measured. "Ms. Whitlock," Margaret Ridgeway said. "We need to speak."

Clara closed her eyes briefly. "About what?"

"About a misunderstanding," Margaret replied. "One that's getting out of hand."

Nimbus's tail flicked. "Panicking."

Clara's voice stayed calm. "I'm listening."

"Come by the house," Margaret said. "Now."

"That won't work for me," Clara replied.

Silence stretched. Then: "You're making this very difficult."

Clara looked at the locked cabinet under the counter, at the space where the brooch should have been all along. "You made it difficult first."

Another pause. Longer.

"Then we'll talk there," Margaret said. "In public."

Clara's pulse ticked up. "That's your choice."

The line went dead.

Nimbus hopped down. "She's moving."

"Yes," Clara said. "And she's scared."

They waited.

Twenty minutes later, the bell chimed.

Margaret Ridgeway stepped inside *Second Chances Antiques* with the posture of a woman used to being received. Her coat was impeccable. Her expression was polite. Her eyes scanned the shop like they were cataloging exits.

Nimbus bristled. "Containment breach."

Margaret stopped at the counter. "You've caused quite a stir."

"I didn't," Clara said evenly. "I noticed one."

Margaret's lips thinned. "You spoke to my daughter."

"I listened," Clara replied.

Margaret folded her hands. "Barbara is sensitive. She imagines things."

The echo flared—sharp, immediate.

Fear.

Calculation.

And beneath it, something brittle and furious.

Clara felt it settle cleanly. This was the one.

"You took the brooch," Clara said quietly.

Margaret's eyes flicked—just once—to the cabinet under the counter.

Then she smiled. "I protected my family."

Nimbus's voice was low. "There it is."

Clara leaned forward slightly. "From what?"

Margaret's composure cracked at the edges. "From scandal. From being torn apart by something that happened decades ago. From losing everything Eleanor built."

"Eleanor built a lie," Clara said.

Margaret's jaw tightened. "She built safety."

Clara shook her head. "She changed a name. You kept paying the price."

Margaret inhaled sharply. "You don't understand what it's like to grow up knowing one truth could undo you."

Clara met her gaze. "You don't understand what it's like to decide who belongs."

Margaret's hands trembled. She clenched them. "I didn't mean for her to die."

Nimbus's ears flattened. "But you pushed."

Margaret's voice broke. "I told her to destroy the brooch. I told her it was too dangerous. She refused." Tears welled, hot and furious. "She said blood mattered more than appearances."

Clara's stomach dropped. "And you confronted her."

"Yes," Margaret said. "I told her I would tell Barbara everything. I told her the truth would come out."

Margaret swallowed hard. "She grabbed her chest. She said she couldn't breathe." Her voice dropped to a whisper. "I froze."

The echo hit—panic spiraling, relief followed by horror.

Clara closed her eyes briefly. "You didn't call for help."

Margaret shook her head, tears spilling now. "I thought... I thought it would pass."

Nimbus's voice was quiet. "It never does."

Clara straightened. "You took the brooch afterward."

Margaret nodded. "I am not the one who took it before she died. I thought Thomas had, but he denied it. Once I knew you had it. I couldn't let it exist. Not with everything it represented."

"Where is it now?" Clara asked.

Margaret looked at the door. "At the house. In the fireplace ash."

Nimbus hissed softly. "Destruction."

Clara's pulse steadied. "Sheriff Halden will need to hear this."

Margaret laughed weakly. "Of course he will."

Sirens wailed faintly in the distance—too coincidental to ignore.

Margaret sank into the chair opposite the counter, shoulders slumping. "I panicked," she said again, like a confession and a plea.

Clara watched her carefully. "That's when people make the worst decisions."

The bell chimed again.

This time, it wasn't cheerful.

It was final.

Chapter Ten

Quiet Confrontation

Sheriff Halden didn't rush in.

That was how Clara knew Margaret Ridgeway had already told him everything.

He stepped into *Second Chances Antiques* with the calm precision of a man who understood that speed was only useful when it was necessary. His jacket was buttoned. His expression was set. Not angry. Not sympathetic.

Resolved.

Nimbus flicked his tail. "Here comes the line."

Halden's eyes moved from Clara to Margaret, who sat rigid in the chair across from the counter, hands folded so tightly her knuckles had gone pale.

"Margaret Ridgeway," Halden said evenly. "Stand up, please."

Margaret didn't argue. She rose slowly, smoothing the front of her coat out of habit more than vanity. Old reflexes. Old training.

"I didn't kill her," Margaret said quietly.

Halden nodded. "I know."

That surprised her. It showed in the way her shoulders loosened just a fraction—just long enough for the truth to settle in.

"You confronted her," Halden continued. "You threatened to reveal the adoption. You caused a stress event that led to cardiac failure. And you failed to call for help."

Margaret closed her eyes. "Yes."

Nimbus's voice was low. "Clean. Clinical. Inescapable. The same as Carl Benton."

Halden pulled out a pair of cuffs but didn't raise them yet. "There's also the matter of evidence tampering."

Margaret's breath hitched. "The brooch?"

"Yes," Halden said. "Destruction of potential evidence."

Margaret nodded again, tears slipping free. "I was trying to protect my daughter."

Halden met her gaze. "You were trying to protect a version of your family that no longer existed."

That landed harder than accusation.

Clara stood quietly behind the counter, heart steady but heavy. This was the part people imagined when they talked about justice—but it never looked the way they expected. No shouting. No collapse. Just a narrowing of options until the truth had nowhere left to go.

Halden stepped closer and gently took Margaret's wrists. The cuffs closed with a soft, final click.

Margaret didn't flinch.

"I loved my mother," she said hoarsely.

"I believe you," Halden replied.

Nimbus watched as Halden guided Margaret toward the door. "That's the thing," he murmured. "Love doesn't stop damage."

At the threshold, Margaret paused and looked back at Clara.

"You didn't have to do this," she said.

Clara met her eyes. "Neither did you."

Margaret nodded once, accepting that.

Halden escorted her out into the square, where the town had already begun to gather—drawn by sirens, by instinct, by the unmistakable scent of consequence.

The door closed behind them.

The shop felt different now.

Not lighter.

Not safer.

Clearer.

Nimbus jumped down from the counter and padded over to Clara, brushing against her leg. "That's two."

"Yes," Clara said quietly.

Nimbus tilted his head. "Are you noticing the pattern?"

Clara looked around her shop—the antiques, the quiet, the objects that held more truth than people liked to admit.

"Yes," she said. "Silence doesn't keep people safe."

Nimbus's tail flicked. "It just delays the damage."

Outside, voices rose and fell. The town was recalibrating again, searching for the right words to explain what had just happened.

Clara knew what they would choose.

Unfortunate.

Tragic.

Complicated.

Anything but honest.

She turned off one of the lamps, then another, letting shadows reclaim the corners of the shop.

Because the truth had done its work.

And Briar Hollow would never quite forgive her for it.

Chapter Eleven

What the Town Calls Loyalty

B riar Hollow did not argue with the arrest.

It absorbed it.

Clara saw it happen in real time—from the shop window, from the corner of the square, from the way people adjusted their posture as Sheriff Halden's cruiser pulled away with Margaret Ridgeway in the back seat.

No shouting.

No protests.

Just a collective tightening.

Nimbus sat in the front window, tail wrapped neatly around his paws. "They're deciding what this costs them."

Clara didn't look away. "They already know."

The first response came in casseroles.

Three of them, delivered within an hour. Wrapped carefully. Labeled with neat handwriting. No notes inside—just food and the expectation that gratitude would smooth the moment.

Clara stacked them in the back room without opening a single lid.

Then came the silences.

Mrs. Calder crossed the street instead of passing the shop window. The man who always bought postcards pretended to take a phone call when he saw Clara unlocking the door. The florist delivered arrangements to every Ridgeway cousin except Barbara.

June stopped by near closing time, leaning against the counter instead of sitting.

"They're calling it complicated," she said.

Clara nodded. "They always do."

June studied her. "Some people think you went too far."

Nimbus's ears twitched. "There it is."

"And others?" Clara asked.

June exhaled. "Others are relieved. Quietly. They won't say it where it carries."

Clara absorbed that. "And you?"

June smiled thinly. "I'm tired of pretending quiet equals kind."

That mattered more than any casserole.

After June left, Clara closed early. Again. The town would survive without her for a night.

She locked the door and leaned back against it, feeling the echo of the day settle into her bones. Not fear this time. Something heavier.

Cost.

Nimbus padded over and looked up at her. "You're paying it."

"Yes," Clara said. "They won't forget."

Nimbus's tail flicked. "Good. That means they'll remember what happens when they try."

Clara turned off the overhead lights, leaving only the soft glow of the lamps. The antiques watched her from their shelves, witnesses without judgment.

She moved to the counter and opened the cabinet beneath it—empty now. The brooch was gone. Destroyed. Reduced to ash and intention.

But its echo lingered anyway.

Protection.

Pride.

Fear.

Clara closed the cabinet and straightened.

Outside, Briar Hollow continued to practice normalcy. Laughter drifted from the diner. A car radio played too loud. Life went on the way it always did—around the truth, not through it.

Nimbus jumped onto the counter and curled beside her. "They'll be colder now."

Clara nodded. "Yes."

Nimbus yawned. "That's the price of not lying."

Clara looked out at the square one last time before pulling the shade.

She hadn't fixed the town.

She hadn't saved everyone.

But she'd drawn a line.

And Briar Hollow now knew exactly where it was.

Chapter Twelve

What Blood
Leaves Behind

T he object arrived two days later.

Not with drama.

Not with a knock.

It was waiting on the shop counter when Clara unlocked the door in the morning—placed neatly between the brass lamp and the stack of vintage postcards like it had always belonged there.

Clara froze.

Nimbus, already alert, stiffened. "That's new."

"Yes," Clara said quietly. "And it wasn't there when I locked up."

Nimbus raised a paw a counted three claws, "That's three times now that locked door didn't stay locked. When the brooch package arrived, when Margaret Ridgeway took it back, and now this thing."

The shop showed no signs of forced entry. No broken latch. No disturbed dust. Whoever had come in had known exactly how to do it—or hadn't needed to try at all.

Clara didn't touch the object yet.

She didn't need to.

The echo pressed outward, subtle but unmistakable.

Recognition.

Approval.

Expectation.

Nimbus's tail flicked once. "That's not a threat."

"No," Clara said. "It's an acknowledgment."

The object itself was unremarkable at first glance: a narrow leather folio, the kind used for documents or photographs. Well-worn, but cared for. The clasp was intact. The leather smelled faintly of smoke and old paper.

Clara slipped on her gloves.

Inside the folio were photographs.

Old ones.

Black-and-white. Sepia. Carefully arranged.

Families.

Not just one.

Clara's breath slowed as she turned the first photograph over.

A familiar face stared back at her—Eleanor Ridgeway, younger than she'd ever seen her, standing beside a woman whose features mirrored her own. Between them, a baby wrapped in a blanket.

On the back, written in careful script:

Protected.

Clara turned the next photograph.

Another town. Another family. Another baby. Different names. Same posture. Same hands.

Same decision.

Nimbus's voice dropped. "That's not one secret."

"No," Clara said. "It's a pattern."

The final photograph lay beneath the others, heavier somehow despite being the same size.

A recent one.

Taken from a distance.

Clara.

Standing in her shop doorway.

Looking up at something she couldn't see.

Her pulse spiked, then steadied.

Nimbus's ears flattened. "They're watching you."

"Yes," Clara said. "But they're not stopping me."

She closed the folio carefully and set it on the counter, hands steady now.

Someone had been keeping track—not just of objects, not just of secrets, but of *her*.

Not to threaten.

To evaluate.

To see whether she would look away.

Clara glanced toward the front window. Briar Hollow moved as it always did—cars passing, people talking, normalcy resuming its practiced rhythm.

But she knew better now.

This wasn't just a town problem.

It never had been.

Nimbus hopped onto the counter and sat beside the folio, eyes bright. "You passed."

Clara met his gaze. "A test."

Nimbus's tail flicked. "Congratulations. You're interesting."

Clara exhaled slowly and turned the sign to **OPEN**.

Because whatever blood tried to keep quiet—

Whatever families tried to bury—

Whatever patterns had been hiding in plain sight—

She wasn't done listening.

And whoever had sent the folio?

They'd just told her exactly how much larger the truth was than Briar Hollow.

Continue the Quiet Discretion Mysteries

Briar Hollow doesn't stay quiet for long.

If you enjoyed these stories, the next mystery awaits in **Book Four: *Quiet Inheritance in Briar Hollow*.**

Each installment features a complete mystery, while Clara Whitlock's story continues quietly in the background.

Reading Order

The next chapter of the Quiet Discretion Mysteries is already unfolding.

A Small Favor

If you enjoyed these stories, a brief review helps other readers discover the series.

Even a sentence or two is appreciated. Thank you for reading.

About the author

Petra Shaw writes quiet, character-driven cozy mysteries with a gentle paranormal edge.

Her stories are set in small towns where secrets linger, objects hold memories, and truth often waits for someone willing to notice what others overlook. With a focus on atmosphere, intuition, and understated suspense, Petra's books favor thoughtful mysteries over shock—and resolution over chaos.

When she isn't writing, Petra can usually be found imagining new towns, new silences, and the next mystery waiting just beneath the surface.

Meet Petra Shaw the Author of Paranormal Cozy Mysteries

Petra Shaw

www.ingramcontent.com/pod-product-compliance
Lightning Source LLC
Chambersburg PA
CBHW011436240626
47153CB00011B/3017